EL NUEVO MUNDO
BRIAN YAPKO

EL NUEVO MUNDO
BRIAN YAPKO

Queer Space
New Orleans

Published in the United States of America and United Kingdom by
Queer Space
A Rebel Satori Imprint
www.rebelsatoripress.com

Paperback ISBN: 978-1-60864-206-9
Ebook ISBN: 978-1-60864-207-6
Library of Congress Control Number: 2022935207

CONTENTS

PART I: THE WRITER

There's water in the *acequia* – the old Spanish irrigation canal that flows across the street from our house. It runs like a ditch on the other side of Aguas Dolores. Normally water would be a good thing since Santa Fe can be as dry as bone. Normally, water means relief from New Mexico's frequent plagues of drought. It means the fresh scents of juniper and piñon. It means the aspens will turn gold instead of papery dead brown. To each gaunt coyote, bobcat, and roadrunner it means life itself. Rain is a good thing.

But not if it means that flood waters will cascade down from the Sangre de Cristos. Not if it means that swollen rivers from the nearby Rockies will release tsunami waves which viciously destroy all objects in their path, pulling flailing pedestrians underwater to their deaths on Canyon Road. Not if the rain presages the coming of the Deluge – that great drowning which may represent either our punishment – or our salvation.

I realize this probably sounds like unnecessary hysteria. But I'm a drama queen. And I tell you ... the rain is pounding on the roof like a hundred drums of doom. When I look up from my antique oaken desk, I see clouds the color of charcoal obscuring the Sangres. It makes me shudder. What makes this rain unusual? It's not like we don't have weather in New Mexico. Hell, at 7,000 feet, Santa Fe is high enough up for us to get snow on Halloween. What's so strange about rain on the

Dia de los Muertos? Why is this storm different from all other storms?

Breathe, Nick. *Ay,* my hand is shaking. I have to stop staring at the sky. There's nothing to see up there but black and grey and the occasional flash of lightning. And if there *is* anything terrifying up there beyond the clouds... well, *gracias a Dios,* I can't see it. It's outside the picture frame. A good thing, too, because everything I *do* see right now seems so strange. The sky is strange. The mountains. The houses on the street. The tendons and veins in my writing hand. Daniel. All of it.

Everything before me now carries Astra's retributive signature. That insistent pounding rain on our flat roof? By Astra. The angry black clouds above us? Astra. That flock of swallows flying south? Well, it's the 1st of November. They'd be flying south to Mexico anyway, right? Or was this moment also brought to us by...? Astra de la Luz. Who the hell was she really? A brilliant but obscure artist? A good but peevish friend? Just an old lady? Or how about this: an exotic alien being who brought war to Earth from a distant world? You think I'm joking. I'm not.

That loud crashing of thunder! I feel like I'm going to pass out every time I hear it. I cover my ears with my hands, but only for a few seconds because I need to hear what Daniel is doing. I can hear his clattering in the *casita*. This morning, he's dividing his time between painting and rearranging the materials and equipment in his studio. Marble and bronze – hellishly heavy to move – must get pushed to the side. Chisels, saws and sandpaper get put on the shelf. After years of working only with stone and metal, extraordinary circumstances have forced him to put aside sculpting. Painting has now become his number one priority.

Since Saturday afternoon – that was two days ago – Daniel has been painting like a madman. A supremely talented madman. I was reassured when I saw his first painting. It's an oil on canvas depicting

2

our own street here in Santa Fe with our own updated pueblo front-and-center – the most logical subject for him to start with. He created a beautiful landscape: cobalt for the sky, canary yellow sunlight, ochre for the adobe houses, gold for the aspen which flutter outside our living room window. The painting is finished off with crimson and lilac-colored flowers. Best of all, there isn't a cloud in the sky. And, of course, there is his name signed with a modest flourish in the lower right corner: Daniel Vigil Cruz. *Nuestra Calle* – Our Street – was exactly what I hoped to see. It makes me breathe a little easier.

But understand something. I can't tell Daniel what to paint – his gift doesn't work that way. To be fair, he has asked me to make a list of the things I'd like to see him capture on canvas. But we both know it's all subject to his artistic inspiration.

Astra was right in the end. She always knew Daniel would be a great painter. Up until Saturday, I'd only ever known him with a chisel or hammer in his hand. And understand: what Daniel sculpts is first-rate. We have two of his bronze sculptures sitting on our front lawn. Sometimes tourists detour up from Canyon Road to drive by and take pictures.

But now I picture his sculptures anchored at the bottom of some salty sea, surrounded by frigid, watery silence. I think of those ancient Egyptian statues of Isis and Horus that divers have found in the Mediterranean near Alexandria. Or the marble Caesars that marine archaeologists pull from the Bay of Naples. Or the pre-Columbian artifacts drowned in the *cenotes* of Yucatan...

I told Daniel about this morbid, underwater fantasy – his beautiful artworks lost at the bottom of the sea. He stopped mid-stroke and put his paintbrush down. He walked over to me, lifted up my trembling chin, looked deep into my eyes and kissed me hard on the lips. "That

3

won't happen, corazón" he whispered. Then he offered me a grim smile and said he had to get back to work.

Do I dare believe him? Do I have the *courage* to believe him? How can he be so sure? Artists! I wonder what he's painting now?

Oh Daniel, damn you! I can't live like this! Why am I even bothering to write these words down? Who on Earth will ever read this journal? Yes, I know. No one can really say what the future holds. I can't see the big picture. I have neither the wisdom to count the clouds nor do I know who is tipping the water jars of heaven. All I know is that it's raining hard, there's water in the *acequia*, and maybe it's important for there to be a record. That's the point of this journal.

My journal. Belonging to me, Nicholas Clements. Today's date: November 1, 2066. As I mentioned, it's the Mexican Day of the Dead. If Astra hadn't died, if the storm hadn't come upon us, if Daniel and I hadn't stepped into the pages of some science fiction horror story, we'd be celebrating the *Dia de los Muertos* in the Plaza. We bought costumes and everything – a sexy gladiator costume for Daniel, a bullfighter costume for me, complete with red scarf. But the fiesta organizers announced that it was being cancelled due to "inclement weather." What an understatement!

I have trouble picturing the Plaza under water. Would the Spanish flags at the Palace of the Governors ebb and flow like krill in the ocean currents? Would the great bells of the Cathedral of St. Francis corrode in the salty water, turning green and silent?

I realize that this must sound pretty elegiac. It's just that... Well, Santa Fe was a good place for Daniel and me to move to. Venerable at over 400 years old. Creative. The City of Artists. Above all, it was peaceful – a welcome backwater after we had tired of big city chaos. We've been here for twelve years, since 2054. We met in San Francisco

4

about one year before that.

Another crash of thunder! Will I ever get used to this? Oh, Daniel! Can't you make this stop?! How my heart is pounding!

* * *

Bien. I'm having some tea. I'm relatively calm, semi- collected and ready to write.

So. Daniel and I met in 2053. When we first got together I was a nobody, really – a nerdy 23 year-old kid, skinny, average-looking and recently possessed of a uniquely unlucrative degree in art history. I had a Spanglish background –¡la verdad !– with an Anglo dad and a Mexican mother, both dedicated Catholics who were hard- working and frequently angry that I wasn't a tough, manly boy like my four brothers.

We lived in the Latino section of Pasadena where you asked questions in English and they were answered in Spanish. I bounced between religious and public schools. I hated sports, I didn't have many friends but I loved to draw and look at pictures of fine art. Pasadena was boring, but between the Huntington and the Norton Simon it had some great museums.

In fact, the art scene was the only good part about my life in SoCal. You've probably already guessed that my parents were pretty narrowminded. From the time I was a little boy, they wanted me to marry Lorna Sanchez, the pretty daughter of a family friend. Afraid to rock the boat, I led Lorna on for years– through high school and into our twenties -- pretending to enjoy a sexless kiss here and there but, unless drunk, utterly incapable of following through. I stayed in that miserable little closet until an easy-going art major at Cal State with a quick smile and sparkling eyes named Tomás set me free. After months of sneaking about, Tomás and I were discovered fooling around together in our tool shed by my parents and Lorna, who had been planning a birthday surprise. Well, the surprise was on them. The fall-out was bridge-burning. After saying things that no parent should ever say to a son, my parents disowned me. Lorna, who I truly cared about as a friend, spit in my face and walked out of my life. My years of lying – to my parents, to Lorna and to myself – had availed no one.

Tomás and I graduated from college and moved to San Francisco together. Then he met a gym-sculpted lawyer with a BMW named Julian and we broke up. So there I was, alone in the City on the Bay. I discovered the Castro District and also began to flirt with the San Francisco art scene. Despite my degree, I had no artistic talent to speak of, so I got good at being a substitute teacher. That's what gave me a paycheck. But my real calling was as a freelance writer. I earned extra money by writing reviews of art exhibits for rags and internet art sites. That's how I met Daniel.

Daniel Vigil Cruz. Just for a minute I want you to forget about the Deluge and the apocalyptic drowning of sculptures and humans. I want you to see Daniel through my eyes – the good and the bad – so you can understand the decisions that I've made.

Back in 2053, Daniel Vigil Cruz was known in San Francisco art circles as *El Escultor* – the Sculptor. I first heard of him when I was out having a *cerveza* with my new friend, Jen, at the Sisterhood Bar in the Mission District. She was an insider in the gallery scene. Knowing about my own Latino background, she was excited to share with me about Daniel. *El Escultor* had arrived in San Francisco two years earlier from some obscure village in Mexico and had secured a remarkable reputation with astonishing speed. The word in the gallery circuit was that Daniel Vigil Cruz possessed a rare talent which was coupled with a rare beauty that made him irresistible to men and women alike. No one could guess whether he was gay or straight. They said that he dated no one, that he was married only to his work. Everything I heard about him intrigued me. I looked for him on the internet. There was information about some of his sculptures but nothing about him personally – not even a picture. I had to meet him!

When I found out that *El Escultor* was the featured artist at a gallery-opening near Union Square I wrangled a press invitation. Many glitterati of San Francisco's art world were there. I was dazzled. The gallery was packed with people dressed to the nines and making the pretentious small-talk so common in the art world. Jen cancelled on me at the last minute, so I was left there without knowing a soul and feeling very out of place. There was an open bar at the front entrance but I ignored it. Whatever happened this evening, I wanted my mind to be clear.

When I walked into the gallery's great room it was dominated by three of *El Escultor's* newest larger-than-life sculptures. The first one was a modern bronze and aluminum metallic origami called *The Phoenix* which, though fascinating, was too abstract and just wasn't my cup of tea. I liked the second piece better. It was a hybrid marble and steel piece, a really interesting, stylized *pas de deux* of two ballet dancers – ambiguous in gender – presented with a stunning sense of flying motion. This one impressed me. It was as if Rodin had somehow captured Bernini's gift for movement.

But it was the third statue which blew me away. It was a male nude, chiseled out of marble. It had the heroic quality of Greco-Roman-Renaissance art – but with some contemporary twists. This nude man, stunningly proportioned, was seated on a narrow marble bench. His angular facial features struck me as Latino – almost Aztec. His pose was relaxed, his head tilted back slightly, his mouth open. His back and chest muscles were well-defined. He had a marble chain around his neck. A stone pendant appeared to dangle from it onto his bare chest – an object which recalled a cross, but which bore extra beams and strange markings. Graceful stone fingers powered by a muscular forearm strummed a stone guitar which rested on an upraised bare thigh. The marble guitar pressed against, but did not obscure, the subject's relaxed but still-impressive manhood. Unconcerned by his own nudity, the subject appeared to be serenading someone with a tender mariachi love song. The sculpture was titled *El Hombre Que Canta* – The Singing Man. The raw sensual power of this statue coupled with its filigreed delicacy stunned me. My jaw dropped at its perfection. It caught my breath like no artwork I've seen before or since.

As I was staring at the statue my attention was directed to a commotion beyond it. There against a wall painted green and yellow was a young man who was being photographed by patrons and media alike. So that was Daniel Vigil Cruz! Dressed in a stylish amber-hued glam-suit, he was posing in between two of his bronze wall sculptures. And while I had been staring at the statue, he had been staring at me.

Judging by his appearance, Daniel was just a bit older than me but – given the way he dressed, the way he carried himself – he seemed infinitely more sophisticated. I couldn't take my eyes off of him. All of the gossip had been true. He was a lean, swarthy *hombre*, probably in his mid-twenties with killer looks. He was about six feet tall, which was two inches taller than me. He had sparkling brown eyes with just a hint of amber. For a moment I was confused – I felt like I had seen him before. Then I looked from Daniel back to his sculpture and smiled. There were some differences, but it was obvious that he himself had been the model for *El Hombre Que Canta*!

I was 23 years old. After some embarrassing fumblings with Lorna and some real heat with Tomás, I wasn't exactly a virgin. But when

Daniel gazed at me from the other side of *El Hombre Que Canta*, across that crowded room full of patrons, critics, cocktails and photographers, he aroused me – visibly – like no man ever had. Flustered, I removed my jacket and held it in front of me lest my pulsing enthusiasm for the artist become too obvious. When Daniel saw this, he grinned and winked at me. But believe me, I was having way more than just a powerful sexual reaction. I got butterflies in my stomach; my knees went weak. Time stood still. Then, ignoring the questions people were asking and the cameras that were directed at him, and without ever breaking eye contact, Daniel started walking towards me...

Until I die, I will never forget that day. September 22, 2053. That's our anniversary. Each September 22nd since then we drink champagne, laugh about our lives together, look at old pictures and make passionate love as if we were twenty again. Daniel Vigil Cruz. The scent of him. Watching him sleep. Watching him shave in the morning without even the modesty of a towel. The sight of him has never failed to make my pulse race. Now more than ever, I must ask: what mystery makes this type of love possible? This all-consuming love that would risk anything and everything to be together? *Ay de me*, if I knew then what I know now would I have turned and walked away before getting involved with him?

Not a chance. I would still have been drawn to him. Don't get the impression that his beauty put me under some strange erotic spell. And it's not just that Daniel is so suave (how he hates it when I embarrass him with compliments like that!) And it's not just that he's brilliantly talented. You know what it is? It's that Daniel, for all of his – how shall I say it? – his *strangeness*, is incredibly decent. Unlike Astra – or me – his sense of justice is unusually nuanced. Quite simply, he's the best individual I've ever known. I say this with both of my eyes open. I say it

9

despite every massive lie he's ever told me, despite all he's been through, and despite everything that's yet to come. I forgive it all because... *Bien,* because Daniel is better far than I will ever be.

Let me go back to the night we met. When Daniel joined me in front of *El Hombre Que Canta,* he introduced himself. Then he took my jacket out of my trembling hands and placed it on a chair. Seeing that I was still in an elevated mood, he smiled, took my hand, raised it to his lips and then whispered in my ear that my physical arousal was no source of shame. To the contrary. Touching my arm and then adjusting some stray hairs on my head, he said that the feeling was definitely mutual. He spoke in a low baritone voice that had the slightest hint of a classical Spanish accent. I was astonished at the liberties he was taking. I should have been indignant but when I tried to say something I stammered and actually felt even more drawn to him. Then he invited me to dinner for the following evening. Of course I said yes. Daniel said *"perfecto."* He kissed me familiarly on the cheek and then disappeared into the crowd. I was left like Cinderella touching my cheek in stupefied wonder at the attentions of Prince Charming.

The next evening, Daniel picked me up at my apartment in Noe Valley promptly at 7:00. He brought me red roses, bowed as if he were a courtly gentleman from another age, and again took my hand and put it to his lips. He was much more subdued than he had been the night before. Shy, even. He apologized for being so direct at the gallery. I shrugged. I didn't mind. He said that he had to play a certain role at these openings. He didn't really enjoy it, but it was necessary. He would rather spend quiet time with just one person. What he wanted above all things was a simple life with someone who he truly loved and who loved him back. No illusions. That sounded good to me.

He took me to El Conquistador where we sipped wine and talked for hours. I could barely eat because I was so attracted to him. After dinner we ditched his car and went for a long walk to his apartment in the Mission District. As soon as we entered that immaculate Victorian apartment our lips locked together. We stayed that way for hours in various states of dress.

Later on, I remember lying in bed with him, our skin still warming the sheets. He reached for me but instead of my lips, he kissed my chest and then my forehead as if he were blessing me. In a low voice he said that it was what was in my heart and mind that attracted him. He made me giddy. Nobody had ever talked to me that way before.

Then Daniel jumped out of bed, wrapped a towel around his waist, threw one to me as well and pulled me from the bed to show me his collection of art. It was magnificent! He had pottery from Oaxaca, silver work from Taxco. He had a couple of Pueblo-style vases that were from Santa Fe, New Mexico – that's where he told me he was originally from – and on his wall he displayed paintings that dated back to the 19th and 20th Centuries, including two Chagalls and a Miró, He showed me a small model of two nudes that he had made based on a Bernini. And he showed me a very handsome oil portrait of him by an obscure painter in Santa Fe. It had a memorably spiritual quality – in it Daniel appeared serenely happy. The artist's name scrawled in the lower left was "de la Luz". Someone I'd never heard of.

Daniel loved that I knew so much art history. Yet, even without any university training, Daniel's knowledge far exceeded my own. He could have written a master's thesis on three millennia of sculpture, from Polyclitus to Donatello to Rodin. In my view, Daniel's talent ranks up there with each of these masters. I first fell in love with *El Hombre Que Canta* and some of his other works. Then I fell in love with the sensitive man wrapped only in a loin towel who now proudly showed

11

me his art. What I loved most was that Daniel was utterly oblivious to the fact that his own beauty overwhelmed everything else he showed me. How could I not fall deeply in love with him?

We were married within a year. If you can believe it, I'm the one who asked. He was startled by my proposal since he was always the assertive one. He asked me if I was sure. I said I was never so sure of anything in my life. I asked him again: "Daniel, will you marry me?" After a long delay he grinned, kissed me and with maddening understatement said "¿*Sí, como no?*"

Marrying Daniel Vigil Cruz has been my one real claim to fame. He will always be *mi amado* – my beloved Daniel – come hell or high water (no irony intended.) But, to be honest, I still don't understand what Daniel saw in me. He talked about my heart and mind, but how does that make me special? I'm neither saint nor genius. I'm certainly no Adonis. But for some reason we were drawn together.

Fast forward to 2066. Daniel is pushing 40 but still trim and handsome as ever. Turning his back on glittering San Francisco life 12 years ago has obviously agreed with him. He says he's never missed that lifestyle, not even once.

As for me, I see myself as a typical boring 36-year-old guy with chestnut hair, hazel eyes, love handles and a small touch of neurosis. But Daniel loves me. He still calls me *guapo* which, improbably, means handsome. I don't think the lies he's told me in the past matter anymore. Whatever horrors the future may hold, it's clear beyond reason that he loves me.

But now that Astra is dead and the world faces extinction, how do *I* feel about *Daniel*? Good question. I love him, of course. I hate him a little too, but overall I love him crazy – *and not because I have no choice.* Besides, his work matters. And I know that I'm important to his work.

12

I have to overlook the differences between us. Marriage is for better or worse, no?

The rain has softened to a drizzle. Good. I don't hear Daniel clattering about the studio anymore. That means he's probably painting again. Also good.

Daniel Vigil Cruz and Nicholas Clements. Oh, and Ariel, our dog – an Australian shepherd with one brown eye and one blue. We live on half an acre at 1453 Calle Aguas Dolores. We have a main house – pueblo revival, of course – along with a *casita* in the back which Daniel uses as his studio. Aguas Dolores is one of the three famous art streets of Santa Fe. You name it, it's here: *modernismo*, Santa Fe Traditional, Navajo, Spanish Colonial, *milenio-nuevo*, Pueblo, Albuquerque kitsch.

El Martillo, Daniel's gallery, features his preferred style, Italian Baroque. Daniel has been working on his own version of Bernini's *Apollo and Daphne* for the last year – the one where Daphne magically transforms into a tree just as Apollo, consumed with desire, is about to catch and ravish her. Only now Daphne is a male. I blushed when Daniel said Apollo was modeled on me. Well, if he could go bare in *El Hombre Que Canta*, I suppose I can handle it in this piece – assuming he eliminates the love handles. But unfortunately, *Apollo and Daphne* will have to remain unfinished. In fact, all of Daniel's sculpting will have to wait. Given the aftermath of Astra's death, painting is what matters.

Alright. That's all you need to know about Daniel and me. In fact, he just walked in. It's only noon and he looks utterly exhausted. I'll get back to this journal in another hour or two. Writing all of this down really helps. Thank you for keeping me sane!

13

A few hours have passed since my prior entry. I'm looking out the window now. The rain turned to hail for about ten minutes and left little ice globules everywhere. The noise was terrifying! Daniel came running in from the *casita* to make sure Ariel and I were alright. *Dios mio*, I get so scared! I want my husband. I know his work is important, but...!

Ay, Nicky, stop this! See what you can get down on paper before dinner.

Esta bien. I've told you all about Daniel and me. Now let me tell you about Astra.

Astra de la Luz was a remarkable old lady. In fact, I had no idea just how remarkable! When she died two days ago, she was probably 80 pounds dripping wet. She lived alone, although we urged her to get someone to stay nights. She wore her long white hair in *trenzas*. She always wore a pair of tinted bifocals which looked like they came from New Mexico Territory days. And she wore flowery Mexican-style blouses with colors so flamboyant she made me jealous. I met her soon after we moved to Santa Fe. As for her and Daniel...

Perdóname. I have to remember to tell this story in sequence. Otherwise you'll never understand. What I can say for right now is this: Daniel knew Astra before I did. Her combined gallery and studio, the Galleria Astra, was right next door to El Martillo, the studio Daniel opened. Both buildings were about a mile from our home up Aguas Dolores. Galleria Astra was a renovated adobe house from the late 1800s. It had been added to in the 20th Century and again in the early 21st. The old part of the house was where Astra lived. The two additions were where she had her studio at the rear, and up front, the gallery which was open to the public. Daniel introduced me after he and Astra had apparently hit it off. I instantly adored her. I've always been partial to eccentric old ladies with vulgar mouths and garish clothes. *Tía* Astra became my friend.

Although Daniel was the artist, it sometimes seemed like Astra was closer to me than to him. Sometimes Daniel complained about her. She respected his work as a sculptor but kept pressing him to take up painting. "Daniel needs to express the soul of the painter!" she would say. She somehow felt that by failing to paint, Daniel was shortchanging his talent and (to use her words) "shackling his soul." Daniel refused. Following Astra's somewhat disingenuous suggestion, I once foolishly asked him to paint something for me – anything. He got so angry with me his eyes blazed. We didn't speak for two days. After that, I never again interfered with his artistic decisions.

Dammit, the thunder is back again! And it sounds terrifyingly close! Ariel is whining that she wants to go out – I have to let her, but only for a minute. The rain will surely turn hard again soon. Those clouds over the Sangre de Cristos... Black as the pits of hell!

I still can't get over how miserably the world has changed since Friday, when this all came to a head. It was the day before Halloween. Just three days ago it was a gorgeous October day -- Santa Fe at its best. Daniel decided to close El Martillo early. He stopped next door to see Astra before coming home. Her gallery had been closed to the public now for over two months, since her illness had begun to cripple her. Daniel said she looked awful but was in a feisty *La Llorona* mood. As weak as she was, she practically pushed him out the door.

Clearly, Astra's condition weighed heavily on him but there was nothing to be done. At this point, it was early afternoon. Daniel and I had a light lunch and then took Ariel for a leisurely walk up Canyon Road – that charming street where dozens of 19th Century pueblos have been converted into galleries. Now they were all decorated for Halloween and *Los Muertos*. The street was rich with pumpkins and

15

calaveras and the smell of roasting *piñons*. The aspen and cottonwood trees shimmered canary yellow and amber.

If that sounds poetic, dear journal, it's because I want to remember it. I don't think there'll ever be another day like it.

We got home around 2:30 p.m. The phone beeped. It was Astra. Daniel answered but she asked for me. He shrugged, his face stony. He handed me the phone. Astra's voice was low and ominous. "*Nicolás, mijo*. It is decided. This will be my last night on Earth. *Ven aquí*. You come."

Astra was dying. She couldn't put off having an important talk with me. I told her Daniel and I would be there in five minutes. She said no. I must come alone. I looked at Daniel. I hated to hurt him but can you say no to a dying woman?

Not knowing her instructions, Daniel put his jacket on and said "Let's go, Nicky. We can be there in two minutes."

As gently as I could, I told Daniel that Astra didn't want him to come. She had something she wanted to tell only me.

Daniel's jaw stuck out just a bit – I could see he was hurt. Still holding his jacket he looked out the window, his eyes reflecting the amber leaves on our aspen. Finally, he put his jacket down and said "I understand. It's her way." He touched my arm briefly. "Kiss her *adiós* for me. I'll be in the studio working on Apollo." He slammed the back door and went out to the *casita*.

I jumped in the car and raced over expecting to find Astra on her deathbed. She had worsened quickly in the last two weeks. Breast cancer is what she told us. Advanced. She said she'd done all of the tests, weighed the treatments and wasn't having it. She was too old to put herself through cures that were worse than the disease. She hated doctors who were always looking for the wrong things in the wrong places. She said she needed to remain in control. She would know down to the

16

hour when she was ready to die.

When I got to Astra's, the front door was locked. I peered in the window. The lights were on but she was nowhere to be seen. I knocked and there was no answer. She was probably in bed. I looked for the key, which was hidden in foil underneath a planter filled with rosemary. I knocked on the heavy oak door again to be polite. Then I let myself into the gallery.

The gallery was a bit creepy – like a haunted museum. Hanging on the walls were some twenty of Astra's paintings, each more brilliant than the last, each one of them strangely alive. Astra had the gift. It's a shame she was barely known in the greater art world - but now I think it was a blessing in disguise. How much worse things would be if someone with her powers had sold herself!

I walked to the 19th Century mid-section of her house, in between her studio and the gallery. The smell here was strange – musty old wood combined with the scents of lotions and ointments known only to the old and infirm. Competing with these was the smell of oil paint and varnish emanating from the studio. The bedroom door was ajar. I peeked in her room calling "Astra." To my surprise, the bed was empty.

Following the smell of paint, I found Astra in her studio. She was sitting on a chair looking cadaverous. There was a purple bruise on her right arm. There were also blotches of paint on her arms and smock (not to mention the floor), but her eyes were bright. There was an easel in the center of the room. A painting sat on it covered by a dropcloth. There was a palette messy with paint on the little table next to her. On it were oils in various shades of blue, black and white.

Astra had obviously been painting and was clearly exhausted. She peered at me through her thick bifocals and then smiled broadly with yellow teeth. I knelt before her and took her hand. She said "*Nicolás, mijo*. As if you were my own grandson."

I stood and took her arm. "Let me help you to bed, *Tía*."

To my astonishment, she ripped my hand from her arm and bellowed, "No! After tonight I can sleep forever. Now I must finish this painting. And then..." she whispered conspiratorially, "I need your help."

"You want me to help you with your painting?"

"Not that. Afterwards... *Nicolás*, *mijo*, I have a story I need to tell you. *Mi historia*. You're a writer. This world of yours will need to know why I painted this." She pointed to the covered easel. "And, *mijo*, it is very important for Danny to know everything I tell you. Tell him, *Nicolás*! *Es muy importante*."

"Why can't you tell him yourself, *Tía*?"

"*Ay*. He hates me, *mijo*. And he fears me. He will never listen. I need you to be Danny's ears."

"He loves you, *Tía* Astra!"

She studied me through drooping eyelids. Softly she said, "I know." She sighed and then coughed painfully. "Danny loves me. And he hates me. And he loves me. *Ay*, enough!"

She started to stand and couldn't do it. Easing back into her chair she nodded at the easel and grunted. "You are a writer, *Nicolás*. You put things down on paper and hope to change the world." She smiled devilishly. "I am like you when I create *una pintura*. I put colors on canvas and I too change the world." She took my hand. "We artists make a difference. We live within the words of Picasso, no? 'Art is the lie that makes people see the truth.' *Verdad, verdad...*" she said softly as if drifting into sleep.

I again took her arm. "I'll take you to your room."

Her eyes fluttered open and she glared daggers at me. "The hell you will! As for your Danny..." she made a dismissive gesture. "Danny wastes his talent. What he does with stone is too literal, too clumsy to make a difference."

That angered me. "Daniel's a brilliant sculptor, *Tía* Astra!"

"*Brillante, sí.* But Danny is afraid of painting. Like a six-year old boy, he fears what might come of it. That's why I speak to him through you. I leave unfinished work. When I die, Danny will have a chance to do something important!"

Astra baffled me. Was this the dementia of imminent death? But she seemed so lucid, carefully gauging my reactions. Slyly, she said "Would you like to see what I'm painting?"

I nodded. "Yes, *Tía.*"

She bared her yellow teeth and said "Too bad! Patience! You'll see my *Pintura Grande* soon enough. You and Danny will see it together in the morning."

"Do you want me to stay the night? Shall I stay until...?"

"No, *mijo.* I want you to make us some coffee and help me into the parlor."

She let me lift her from her chair and walk her to the old part of her house, settling her onto her faded sofa. I made some coffee -- "black as coal" is how she wanted it. I could barely drink mine but appreciated the jolt of caffeine.

She had me sit close and took my hand. "*Nicolás,* we both know I'm dying. This will be my last night on Earth." I bowed my head so she wouldn't see me get teary. But as she continued to speak, I went from teary to horrified.

"Death doesn't bother me. *La muerte?* Bah. What bothers me are the lies I've told you about who I am, where I come from, the danger I've placed you and Danny in. What I hate is the evil of those who would destroy this world and leave your Earth a broken, smoking carcass. What I hate are the corrupt people of this obscure planet who murdered José and sold out your Earth to gain power in a poisoned solar system..."

My jaw dropped. I said, "Whoa, whoa, Astra! You're talking crazy! Slow down! What the devil are you talking about?"

She had worked herself up without realizing how unprepared I was for this bizarre onslaught of confessional science fiction. She said "Ay!" and inhaled deeply. She began to take off her bifocals then seemed to think better of it. She peered at me through the tinted glass and then smiled apologetically. "Let me start over, *mijo*." I nodded. She said "I'm not what you think I am, *Nicolás*. I am not human. That's why I must talk to you."

She *was* demented and this was over my head. I picked up her phone. "I'm calling Daniel right now. He'll come and..."

"No!" she screamed. And then – until the day I die I will never forget what happened next! First, I heard a low humming noise surrounding me. Then, the phone I was holding began to fight me! It became fire hot, then flew from my hand and violently smashed against the wall. I stared at it in astonishment. I hadn't done that! In shock I tried to get out of the parlor but a side table flew across the wooden floor and blocked the arched entry. I heard the bolt of the gallery door lock and then the bolts to the side and back doors as well. Then I felt an invisible power physically force my body into the chair across from Astra. I tried to fight, but I couldn't control my own body! I had become a puppet. I have never been so terrified in my life! A poltergeist? Demons? Was Astra a witch? I didn't know what to do or think. I screamed "Stop this! I'm your friend!"

The humming noise stopped at once. Astra looked at me sheepishly. "I'm sorry, *mijo*. I didn't mean to scare you. It's just that you wouldn't

20

believe me. And now, maybe, you will."

I stared at her. Either I was going quite insane or this frail old lady possessed a supernatural ability I had never suspected. And if Astra had the power of telekinesis what else was she capable of? I tried to work my mouth to ask questions but the only words I could form were "Astra, what do you want me to do?"

"Just listen to me, *mijo*. Hear what an old lady has to say. Tell Danny because it's *muy importante*. And then write it all down to remember me when I'm gone. Can you do that for your *Tía* Astra, *mijo*?"

I nodded stiffly.

She seemed relieved. "*Está bien*." She held up her hand freeing me from the psychic hold she had put on me. She unblocked the living room entry and I heard the door bolts unlock.

I believe I could have left her at that point, but Astra was dying and her words and her powers had raised a mystery that I had to understand before she was silenced forever. Time was running out. I decided to stay.

And then, with death approaching, Astra spoke. She spoke of war and vengeance; of judgment and mercy; of the beauty of space and the ugliness of betrayal. Astra spoke of the strange, magical power of art. I listened to the epic story that was her life for over three hours. I also peppered her with questions. At one point I even asked her to prove that she wasn't human by showing me her true form. She refused and said she didn't have one ounce of energy to waste. "*Mijo*, I have two eyes, two arms, two legs just like you. Bah! Why bother with unimportant things when you and Daniel need to focus on survival!"

Survival! Jesus, if the story she was telling me was true…! By the time she was done my eyes were glazed over and I was hyperventilating.

"Drama queen" she called me. But she smiled affectionately as she said it. "Now go home. Tell Danny everything I've said. Come back in the morning with Danny. Find me, *mijo*. You and Danny must be the ones to find me. Together. *Ay*... and call this number." She handed me a piece of notepaper. "Hectór will know what to do with these old bones."

The last thing she did was press her tissue-paper lips to my cheek and hand me a brown-paper package that she insisted I deliver to Daniel. Maybe I should have wept, but everything Astra told me had left me numb and slightly ill. I wasn't even sure if I should believe her or not.

I was a fool. I should have believed her.

PART II: THE PAINTER

I had to take a break. It's now 3:00 p.m. I tried to close my eyes for just a few minutes... to sleep, perchance to dream, *sabes*? But *Nada*. The hail started again. This time it was hail like the seventh plague! It lasted for a good twenty minutes. There are white drifts against the house that look like snow. But the rain has started up again and the ice is melting fast. Daniel didn't come running to check on me this time. I know I shouldn't take that personally! He has work to do. *Ay de mí*. So do I. I'm a writer. So let me record what happened after I saw Astra alive for that last time.

When I walked out of the Galleria Astra carrying the package for Daniel, I was in a daze. I even forgot the car. No matter. Daniel would drive us back to Astra's in the morning to deal with the aftermath. I wandered home down Aguas Dolores staring at the details of the street I knew so well. Everything and everyone looked alien to me – as if I had never seen them before. Tourists taking pictures of the street art. A middle-aged couple raking leaves. Kids dressed like ghosts and vampires showing off their Halloween costumes one night early.

I kept pace with the sunset. Was it me or was it more intense than normal? The sun was hovering low just over the Jemez Mountains. Rays of amber collided with streaks of rocky mountain purple and (I say this without irony) Martian red. Surely that sun would rise again in the morning... wouldn't it?

I got home but I couldn't bring myself to open the door. I stopped to stare at the sunset's pink reflection on the Sangre de Cristos to the east. "There are more things in heaven and earth..." I whispered, wondering what was behind that unearthly light. Then I walked in.

Daniel was cooking supper. He wiped his hands, came over to me, gave me a kiss and then pressed me to him in a lingering, needy hug. When we separated I could see that his eyes were red. His voice trembled slightly. "I'm glad you're home, *corazón*. Is Astra...?"

"No, Daniel. But it's close. She said we should come to find her in the morning. Together. She seems certain she won't live through the night."

Daniel grabbed his jacket. "Dammit... Watch the stove, *guapo*. I've got to get over there."

I startled him by yanking the jacket from his hand. I was frightened for him. "You can't go, Daniel! She gave very explicit instructions. You don't know what she's capable of! She insists on being alone to finish her work. And I'm supposed to give you ... this." I showed him the package Astra had given me.

I think my outburst stunned him for a little minute. I rarely spoke to him that way, so maybe it was better now if I stayed silent. I lightly touched his arm to reassure him. Then I took hold of his hands and placed into them the package that Astra had given me to deliver. At first he just looked at me with a wounded expression. Then he looked down at the package in his hands. He stared at it for the longest time as if weighing what to do with it.

"Daniel, don't you think you should open it?"

He looked at me gravely. Then he smiled sadly and said "*¿Sí, como no?*" He opened the package and put it on the kitchen table. It was painting materials. Brushes, tubes of paint, linseed oil.

24

Knowing how many times Daniel had rejected the idea of turning painter, Astra had *cojones* to give him this as a good-bye gift. I looked at Daniel apprehensively wondering if he was going to explode and fling the package across the room. But he didn't. Under his breath I simply heard him say "I understand. But I do not accept." He resealed the painting set and placed the package on top of the bookcase.

"Are you going to keep it?" I asked.

Daniel didn't answer me. He walked to the window and looked out at the colors of the twilight.

I tried again. "Astra said you'd know what to do with it."

Daniel said dully, "Yes. I'm sure she did." After another minute he looked at me with an almost hostile expression on his face. "You were there for over four hours, Nick. She must have had a lot to say."

I chose my words carefully. "Yes, Daniel, she did. In fact..." I decided not to mention her controlling me with her mind. "In fact, she did nothing *but* talk. She told me a lot of things – remarkable things – about her life. She said I must share everything she told me with you."

"Hm. Did she say why?"

"No. She was very mysterious." Daniel shrugged. "She also said she had to finish this one last painting - *La Pintura Grande*. She said it was her most important work. She said if she didn't finish it her whole life would be wasted."

Daniel exhaled loudly. "Astra can be a little bit scary."

"I've noticed," I said drily, recalling my strange afternoon.

Then Daniel began to pace. "So what the devil is she painting?"

I shrugged. "She wanted to keep it a secret."

"A secret," Daniel said with an edge of sarcasm. "Imagine that."

After a moment of silence, Daniel went back to the kitchen to attend to our dinner. I followed him. He was so tense. Daniel was not

25

himself. He looked over at me as he stirred the food on the stove. "Did Astra say anything about leaving us her studio?"

I couldn't believe my ears. "Geez! That's really cold, Daniel! You expected me to bring up *inheritance* issues with a dying woman? It's better if she leaves believing that the Galleria Astra will outlive her, no?"

He relaxed a little after I scolded him. "Easy, Nicky. I didn't mean anything by that. It's just that she's alone and we've been her closest companions for twelve years. I thought, maybe..."

Daniel's mouth was moving but all I heard was noise. He sounded like a stranger to me. My encounter with Astra had changed me somehow. I put my hands over my eyes and exhaled. Do I repeat her strange story? Would he believe me? It didn't matter. I had no choice. Something she had planted in me compelled me to tell Daniel everything. Besides – it's what I agreed to. I couldn't violate her trust even if I wanted to – especially with everything I now knew about her.

The noise had stopped. I looked up and saw Daniel studying me. "*¿Que pasó*, Nick? Spill it. This is more than Astra dying, isn't it?"

I sighed deeply. I went over to him and planted a kiss on his head. "Finish cooking, Daniel. After dinner we can sit by the fire and then I'll tell you everything she told me. It's pretty strange. I want to make sure I'm not the one who's *loco*."

Daniel smiled and it was a genuinely kind smile. The weirdness was gone. He said "You'll always be a little *loco, guapo*. That's why I married you."

He gave me a kiss on the cheek. Then another one – hungry this time – on the lips. I said no. Not under these circumstances. He looked deep in my eyes for a moment then smiled sadly. "I know, *guapo*. My feelings are just... sort of all over the place."

I took his hand. "When the time is right, corazón." He nodded.

Then I sat at the kitchen chair and we made small talk as he cooked *chile rellenos*. They were amazing as always but I barely tasted them. He paired them with a fragrant albariño but, to be honest, fancy wine was lost on me. Daniel was the gourmet. I was always more tacos and coke. Still, on a night like this, the fancy wine was welcome in case I needed some liquid courage.

I stared at my glass. I was spinning with random thoughts about all the strangers who have come to New Mexico through the centuries. I read once that West America's first winery was near Santa Fe. When the Jesuits came in the late 1500s, they planted grapes, then fermented them to make sacramental wine for communion.

Transubstantiation. A strange idea which I still remembered from Catholic school. And there was Daniel looking at me anxiously, not comprehending that I was trying to deal with grief, the sting of betrayal, mortal terror and a sense of incredible wonder, all while trying to figure out how I was going to get my husband to believe this *loco* story that I was about to tell him. But Daniel needed to understand the terrifying turn that life on our world was about to take!

I was woolgathering and didn't hear his question. When I asked him to repeat it, he said "I just want to know what you're thinking, *corazón*."

I sighed a little. "I'm thinking, *mi corazón*, that I'd like to sit by the fire and have one more glass of wine – just one – while I tell you what Astra told me."

Daniel half-smiled and said sure. I built a fire in the kiva while he cleared the dishes. He poured me another glass of communion wine. Then he sat in the loveseat with Ariel, looked at me with an inscrutable expression and said "Alright, Nicky. Tell me what Astra said."

I sat on the sofa opposite him. I saw my husband's face reflected in

27

the fire. His eyes took on an amber glow. The irony.

I started out slowly. "Daniel, as crazy as Astra's story may sound, there's a part of me that thinks she told the truth."

Daniel seemed to choose his words carefully. "Nicky, you know I love Astra more than just about anyone. But you have to admit she's an odd duck. You and I are probably the only two people on this planet who actually understand her."

I stared at him. "Funny you should phrase it that way, Daniel." I exhaled slowly, trying to find a starting place. "Well, here goes. You know how Astra said she came here as a war refugee? I always thought she was referring to the NorthAm War." I was, of course, referring to the civil wars that fragmented Mexico and the former U.S. thirty-five years ago. When was it? 2029 to 2032? History is not my strong suit.

"Well, wasn't she?"

I cleared my throat. "Yes and no. She was a war refugee, but that's not the war she fled from. If you believe her." I decided to just blurt it out. "Daniel, you're going to think I'm crazy, or that she's crazy. But listen: Astra says that she's not from our world. I don't mean that in an abstract, cultural way. I mean it literally. She says she is not from Earth. She says she's from another world, another planet."

Daniel stared at me for a good twenty seconds. He seemed to be weighing how to react to this revelation. He fiddled with his hands but then broke out into a soft chuckle which resolved into a crooked grin. "Trick-or-Treat's not until tomorrow, Nicky. But that's cute. If anyone could pass as an alien from Mars or wherever, Astra's the one. So, I take it she arrived in Santa Fe via Roswell?"

I could hardly blame him. "You're mocking me."

"No, *guapo*. Not you. It's her. Do you actually believe her? Nicky... don't you think she was telling you a joke?"

28

"No, Daniel. It was no joke." I hesitated and then spit it out. "Astra showed me powers no human could possess."

A pause. "What powers?" He said this very quietly.

"She used her mind to lift things and put them back. She read my thoughts. She... controlled my body. She made me see things in my head that are... impossible." I tried to hide the fact that my eyes had started to water. "She scared me to the bone, Daniel."

I steeled myself for more of his mocking laughter but Daniel surprised me. He got very quiet. He came over to the sofa, sat next to me and put my head on his shoulder. "Nicky, I'm sorry. I shouldn't have laughed." I clutched at him shaking from the memory of the experience. He wrapped his arm around me and held my head to his chest. As I shook he kept saying "It's ok, it's ok." Finally he said "It's a strange universe we live in. Anything is possible. But Nicky... how can you be sure you didn't imagine any of this?"

He didn't mean to insult me, but I pushed him away and stared him down coldly until he saw how deadly serious I was.

"Alright, *guapo*. I believe you." He got up and went back to his loveseat. "Tell me more."

I took a big swig of my albariño. Then I got up and stood before the kiva facing him as if I were making a presentation in class. I would just state the facts.

"Astra said she loved Earth – *La Tierra*. She said she would save it if she could."

He frowned. "Save it? From what? Did she say Earth is in danger?"

"Apparently, yes, Daniel. But let me finish in order while this is all fresh. Astra said she was not born here. She said that I would be her witness and that this would be her testimony. She said that her actions would require explaining – particularly *La Pintura Grande*. She said I

29

was the one she needed to share her story with. I asked her 'What about Daniel?'"

Daniel leaned forward. "And... what did she say?"

I looked down at the rug. "I don't want to hurt you, Daniel. But she said you wouldn't listen. She said that you hated her as much as you loved her. She, um, said you were weak. Her word was *débiles*. That you'd need an extra push to become yourself. She said that I should be your ears and share this story with you. She said that in the morning we had to find her together. Astra de la Luz and her last painting."

Daniel took a long time digesting this. I could see how upset he was. He grabbed the phone. I shouted, "Put it down! You are not calling her, Daniel! We have to follow her instructions to the letter!"

He seemed surprised by my raised voice, but I had to put my foot down.

"Daniel, just sit down and let me finish telling you what I have to tell you. It's not that she doesn't love you. It's just that – for reasons which elude me - she feels compelled to turn you into a painter."

He slowly returned to his seat but did not sit. "She's crazy on the subject." He began to pace and then stopped. "Did Astra tell you anything about a painting she might have for me?"

"I want to finish my story, Daniel. But the answer is yes. When she gave me the package for you, she said to tell you that she kept an old painting you had asked about in her bedroom closet. She says it's safe and she wants us to have it." I hesitated. During my afternoon with Astra I had learned that there was more to art than one might realize. "Daniel, is this painting important?

Daniel seemed relieved that this painting was safe. He looked up at the ceiling and then back at me. "Yes, Nicky. Very much so. But I'll tell you about it later. Anyway, get back to Astra and her journey from Mars or wherever she says she came from."

I ignored Daniel's snark and went back to the sofa.

"Astra's not from Mars, Daniel. She's not even from our solar system. Her home planet is located in the constellation Libra." I suddenly realized what perfect sense that made. I blurted out, "Of course! The scales of justice!"

"What are you talking about, Nick?"

"Astra. Her homeworld was in the constellation of Libra."

Daniel drank some wine. "Assuming for the sake of argument that Astra is telling the truth, does this planet have a name?"

"Tlaloc" I said. "The way she pronounced it sounded roughly like 'Tlaloc.'"

Daniel's expression was difficult to read. "Tlaloc" he repeated as he looked out the window. He spoke in a low voice and gave the name a slight Spanish lilt.

"Yes, that's exactly how she said it. Tlaloc. A planet at war. That's why she and other Tlaloceans had to flee. They were refugees from a horrible interplanetary war. Tlaloc was targeted by another planet – Zolteot. Astra described the Zolteots as *muy malvados* – very evil."

Daniel stared into the fire and repeated the name "Zolteot" as well. I thought I heard a hint of disgust in his voice. This subject of interplanetary politics seemed to intrigue him. After a few seconds of staring at the fire, he cleared his throat and asked, "Why was Tlaloc targeted? What did these Zolteots want?"

"Stolen living space," I answered. "The power to abuse. Pleasure in the pain of others. Astra was bitter. She said these were the same things that Earth people seek after."

"Sometimes I think Astra has acid in her veins."

I exhaled loudly. "Yep. Astra can be a witch. Anyway, the Zolteots' population had apparently exploded out of control. They needed planets to spread out into. Specifically, they needed planets that were hot and dry. How did Astra put it? 'Water was poison to them.'"

"Hm. That sounds strange to my ears. Maybe it's different in Zolteot hell, but for we the living, water is life." He relaxed slightly. "I guess the good news is that an ocean planet like Earth is safe."

I looked at him grimly. "No, Daniel. We are *not* safe. But let me get to that."

"What do you mean we're not safe?"

"Let me tell this story the way Astra instructed me."

He stood up. "Nicky, if we're–"

"Daniel, sit down! Astra said that we must trust her. Nothing we can do right now would make a difference anyway. She believes that she's the only one who has that power. And that's assuming that we should even believe any part of her story."

His face turned to stone but he sat down.

"Astra said Tlaloc was similar to Earth. It had a good mix of dry land and vast seas. But once the Zolteots invaded such a planet, they would use monstrous machines that would thin the air until it was no longer breathable. They would siphon off all the water and use it to fuel their desert-building machines. In the end, all life would die. Only the desert would survive. And the Zolteots."

Daniel turned ashen and when he stuttered his Spanish accent became more pronounced. "So they create their own hell. *Dios mío*, that such things could be!" But then he shook off the dark spell. "Nicky, before we go any further, I need to know. Do you believe that Astra was telling you the truth? About this whole story?"

I stared at him silently.

Daniel stood up and tried to make light of what I had just told him.

"Zolteots. Desert builders. Let's assume they exist. Why all this trouble to kill a water planet? Why not just conquer desert planets?"

"Astra wasn't clear on that but suggested that the Zolteots may covet the salt and minerals from the dried-up oceans." I tried to sound casual but faltered. "Why not ask them yourself, Daniel? Astra says that if nothing repulses them, the Zolteot invasion force will be here in a matter of weeks."

Daniel jumped up from the loveseat. His Adam's apple bulged as he swallowed. His whole manner changed. "*Jesús!* Here? They're coming here?" I nodded grimly. He walked to the window and looked out at the rising moon as its light fought against a growing mist which was beginning to obscure it. Then he walked over to the bookcase where he had placed Astra's gift. He picked it up, seemed to weigh it and then put it back. Then I watched him go into the kitchen, pour a glass of wine and down it in one gulp. Then he came back, sat down, sighed deeply and looked at me. He tried to appear casual again but In his eyes I saw worry and love. We worry *because* we love, no? At any rate, I guzzled down the rest of my own glass. I started shaking again but forced myself to stop. More wine was tempting – to hell with the gourmet stuff–but no. If I was to hold it together, I had to stay relatively calm and detached. Plus I needed to be alert as I resumed the story that I had promised to relay to Daniel.

He sighed and looked at me. He even offered a brave smile as if to comfort me. "*Guapo,*" he said gravely, "nothing's going to happen. But if I'm wrong, I want you to know that I love you very much."

I gulped. "Corazón, please don't worry. Nobody's died yet. And repelling the Zolteots is why she said her grand painting, her *Pintura Grande* was so important."

Daniel wasn't listening to me. He stood up again and began pacing

33

before the kiva. I heard him mutter the words "Zolteots" and "impossible". After what I had been through with Astra, I was gratified that he finally took her story seriously – but now maybe too seriously. He was clearly struggling to accept what Astra had told me about this enemy race of aliens. After a minute he stopped and stood in front of where I was sitting with his arms folded. There was a challenging note in his voice. "Explain to me what Astra told you about the connection between her painting and this supposed alien invasion?"

"Astra said I have to tell you her story in sequence, Daniel. She... even if I try, I can't do it any other way." It was the truth. Astra's psychic influence really had followed me home.

Daniel opened his mouth as if to argue, then closed it. He went back to the loveseat muttering "Astra again." Then he said, "I see. *Está bien*. Keep going."

"We have to finish with Tlaloc before we can get to Earth," I said apologetically. "It's very important." Daniel frowned as I continued. "Astra said that the Zolteots targeted Tlaloc to conquer it and turn it into a lifeless desert. In the course of this war, Tlaloc was destroyed."

"The Zolteots destroyed her home planet."

I hesitated. "Well... actually that's not quite how it happened, Daniel."

He looked at me sharply. "What do you mean that's *not* what happened?"

"This is the part that really troubled me. Astra said Tlaloc was *not* destroyed by the Zolteots." I stood up and kneeled before the fireplace so that I faced away from him when I blurted out the next sentence. "Daniel, Tlaloc was destroyed by the Tlaloceans themselves. They decided to destroy their own planet rather than let the Zolteots take it."

I turned around to gauge his reaction. Daniel's mouth was open.

He stuttered again and said "What? She never..." His eyes flashed. Then he became bitterly sarcastic. "¡Brava, Astra! Gutsy move to burn your own fields! That must have really pissed the Zolteots off."

"It did indeed. Astra used the phrase 'The blood hatred of immortal fury.'"

"And what the hell did Astra mean by that?"

"A war of annihilation with no possibility of peace. War in which betrayal was the aggressor's most potent weapon. Betrayal within betrayal within betrayal." I almost felt like Astra was trying to speak through me. I had to get ahold of myself.

Daniel was clearly baffled. "I don't understand, Nicky."

"I'm sorry. Astra's words in my head – they're confusing me." I went to the window and took a deep breath of air. The temperature had dropped. It was getting cold and misty. After I closed the window I was ready to resume. "Betrayal. Astra said that In the century before the planned invasion, the Zolteots began to infiltrate Tlaloc. They blended in with the population to set the stage ensuring that Tlaloc would open its gates to Zolteot."

"The Trojan Horse," Daniel whispered.

"Precisely. The Zolteots manipulated and bribed corrupt Tlaloceans to collaborate with them. Astra spit on her own floor when she described this! Vile pigs she called them. Kapos." Daniel nodded. "These collaborators caused the death of many thousands of good Tlaloceans. The Zolteot strategy was simple but effective. By the time the Zolteot battle cruisers arrived to invade, there would be too few loyal Tlaloceans left to fight."

"Bastards! What kind of hijos del diablo would collaborate with so vile an enemy? Would betray their own people?"

I couldn't have agreed more. I despise perfidy in all of its forms!

35

Normally, if I catch someone lying to me, I... Never mind. Now's not the time.

I cleared my throat and went on. "In the months leading to the final battle, great fear arose in Tlaloc. Rank and file Tlaloceans had no idea how badly they had been compromised. But there were a few brave leaders who knew. Who tried to turn the tide. Who failed."

"Astra... she was one of these brave few?"

"So she says. Tlaloc was ruled by a caste of leaders who were a combination of judges and high priests. Tlaloc had no monarchs, no elected officials. Only this elite caste of Judge-Priests – I can't pronounce the Tlalocean word Astra used for them – who were united in a grand Council. The Judge-Priests were born into this leadership role because they possessed special powers that ordinary Tlaloceans lacked."

There was a long pause. "Our Astra was one of these Judge-Priests."

"Yes."

Daniel leaned forward. "Did she describe these special powers?"

My memory of Astra's telekinetic control of objects—including my body—was still vivid. "Sh-she said that by channeling thoughts a Judge-Priest could manifest things. She could will things into being. She could concentrate her thoughts and cause things to happen."

Daniel said "hm" and looked away from me out the window. Clouds now completely obscured the moon so there was only an inchoate patch of light in a starless sky. It really was getting colder. He went over to the kiva and placed some dry wood in the dying fire. It immediately burst into renewed flame. He sat on the floor looking at it.

After a pause. "You don't believe me, but it's true. I saw her do it with my own eyes, Daniel."

He looked up at me. Suddenly he looked very tired. "I never said I don't believe you, Nicky." Then he looked back at the fire. "How did

36

these Judge-Priests destroy Tlaloc?"

I paused. "They drowned it."

His expression was one of utter bafflement. "They drowned it? How do you drown a planet, Nicky?"

I could still see Astra's parchment skin and *calavera* teeth as she answered this very question. She had looked down into the grounds of her empty coffee cup and said "*El espacio está tan frío como venganza*" Space is as cold as revenge." Then she smiled grimly, her eyes boring into me. "And in space there is much ice." Apparently with the Judge-Priests' ability to manifest things...

Daniel answered his own question. "... the Judge-Priests used their collective powers to pull water from icy comets and meteors and asteroids and pump it into Tlaloc's atmosphere. Once all this water from space saturated the atmosphere, it fell as rain. And then the rain became the Deluge. And so the Judge-Priests of Tlaloc drowned their own planet to keep their enemies from taking it." A long pause as Daniel's grim smile grew increasingly grotesque. "Did I get it right?"

I raised my eyebrows. "You read my mind, Daniel. A very impressive deduction. The Zolteots had the resources to terraform a planet with *some* water. They wanted some ocean because that's what created salt and such. And water fueled their machines. But a planet that was 95% water simply lost all desert potential. That seemed to be the cutoff. The Zolteots didn't have the mental powers that the Judge-Priests had. Astra said that the Zolteots had nothing but the basic laws of physics, undiluted aggression and a complete lack of conscience."

"But drowning the planet... What happened to the people who lived on Tlaloc, Nicky?" There was a sharp edge to his voice. I looked at him helplessly, sighed and said nothing. That very question has haunted me ever since Astra told me her story. When I didn't answer him, he whispered, "*Jesús Cristo...*"

Quietly I said, "I know."

Daniel and I were silent for another minute. Who knew how many souls died on Tlaloc? I know they weren't human and that they died millions of miles away well over a century ago. But I still couldn't help feeling despair for the loss of so many innocents.

Then Daniel observed: "What the Council of Judge-Priests did ... it must have been an agonizing decision."

I exhaled heavily. "I'm sure. It never would have occurred to me that such a thing has happened here on Earth as well. But Astra mentioned Old Holland as one of several examples. Century after century, when faced with annihilation the Dutch opened their dams and flooded their own country rather than allow it to be taken by Spain, the French, the German fascists..."

"Why didn't the Judge-Priests just use their powers to manifest a Tlalocean victory? Or destroy the Zolteot home planet?"

"The Trojan Horse, Daniel. During the century before the invasion, when the Zolteots were infiltrating Tlaloc and buying collaborators by the thousands, these Tlalocean kapos betrayed the Judge-Priests to the Zolteots. Many hundreds were quietly slaughtered. By the time the Judge-Priests understood the extent to which they had been betrayed, it was too late. Their numbers were too small for their powers to reach that deep into space. They lost any ability to attack the Zolteot home planet or the Zolteot fleet. No, at that point Tlaloc was hopelessly trapped like a ship surrounded by pirates. What do you do? Surrender to the pirates? Or do you take your revenge by sinking the ship to deprive the pirates of their prize?" I ended up asking that a little more forcefully than I had intended.

Daniel swallowed. "I suppose it depends on whether you hate the pirates more than you love the ship."

I shivered a bit. "No, Daniel. There's more to it than that! You should have seen Astra's face when she described the horrific choice they had to make! Look. What if the pirates intended to slaughter everyone that you loved on that ship? And what if your ship was then to be mutilated into a lifeless hulk? ¿Qué haces? ¿Dios mío, qué haces?!" I found myself channeling Astra's tearful plea with me to understand the Judge-Priests' painful decision.

Daniel lifted his hands up helplessly. I could see the fire from the kiva reflected in his eyes. Finally he sighed heavily and said "What would anyone do at that point? I... I guess I'd sink the ship. But I'd pray from the bottom of my soul never to have to face such a decision!"

We were silent for a long time. Ariel stretched and went to lay down by the fire. I got up for some water. When I came back I saw that Daniel hadn't moved an inch. "I need to hear the rest of this, Nicky," he said.

I took a deep breath. "I know. Well, once the flooding of Tlaloc began, the small fraction of Tlaloceans who could, fled the planet to find a new home. And to escape the wrath of the Zolteots. The Zolteots were enraged, you see. The pirates had lost their prize. And the Tlalocean crew who had sunk the ship had escaped through their fingers."

"Ah. 'The blood hatred of immortal fury,'" Daniel murmured.

"At this point, blood hatred on both sides. Yes. But on the Zolteot side this blood hatred was especially directed at the surviving Judge-Priests. That meant Astra. That also meant Astra's husband."

"Astra almost never talks about her married life."

"And yet she told me she had a long, happy marriage to her husband, José. Did she ever mention him to you, Daniel?"

Daniel started to say something but stopped. Instead, he walked over to the window and looked out without answering me.

39

"Daniel," I said. "Are you listening to me?"

"I am, corazón, I am. It's just that... this is all so overwhelming." At that moment we both heard some pattering on the roof. He looked up at the ceiling. "Nicky, is it starting to rain?"

I shrugged. "It wasn't in the forecast, but it sounds like it. Anyway, Astra and José went on the run as high-level refugees from Tlaloc. They had to find a new home and go into hiding because they were being hunted by the Zolteots."

"Did Astra say why they chose Earth of all places?"

"There were a dozen suitable planets within 100 light years of Tlaloc. Earth was the farthest and so, they decided, the safest. Plus, Astra said, it was similar to Tlaloc. In the end, they chose northern New Mexico because this part of Earth most resembled their old home – dry but with rain and rivers enough. The right altitude and somewhat off the grid. They zeroed in on Santa Fe for the same reason we did: because of the art scene. Like all Judge-Priests, Astra and José were artists. On Tlaloc, art was the union of their religion and law. It was the vehicle through which they enforced their judgments. Where better for Astra and Jose to blend in than Santa Fe–the City Different–where everyone is an artist?"

Daniel made a guttural sound which surprised me. This was obviously too much for him.

"What's wrong?" I asked. He didn't answer me. "Daniel, are you alright?"

To my surprise, he blurted out a rant of forceful words. "Nick, I can't listen to this anymore. It's too much. Astra, Tlaloc, an imminent invasion by monster aliens. How far can she push me? I've been an artist my whole life, Nicky. Ever since I was a little boy, I started making clay pottery and fashioning things out of scrap metal. I've studied with the best in México, in New York, San Francisco, here in Nuevo México—I can't stand hearing Astra's..." He flung up his hands. "*Mierda*. Bullshit. Even if she's dying. She paints so she wants me to paint. *Ella quiere...* She wants to save the world with a painting. Her painting is her religion. ¡*Dios... Dios!* I'm tired, Nicky. I'm really tired." He ran his fingers through his hair and then buried his face in his hands.

His barrage of words utterly confounded me. It was completely off-topic from what I had been saying. Maybe this was too much for him? I went over to him and pressed his head against my chest. He wrapped his arms around me and we just stayed that way for a few seconds. Finally he put both hands on my chest and pushed me away. "I'm sorry I'm a little high strung, Nicky. Astra's dying and..." He made a gesture of helplessness.

"I know."

"Nicky...?"

"What, corazón?"

"Art *is* important. But it's not about law, or religion, or judgment. It's an expression of the soul. Artists are interpreters. We aren't God, not one of us."

"I never said that. Why are you getting upset? That's just what Astra said."

"I know." He muttered, "Astra. Arrogant Astra."

I looked at Daniel appraisingly. "She was right, wasn't she? What she said about you. You love her and you hate her."

"Get back to your story, Nicky" he said mechanically. "Astra and José. When did she tell you they arrived? During the 30s? After the NorthAm War?"

"Not the 2030s, Daniel. According to Astra, they arrived on Earth during the late 1930s. Right before World War II."

41

"She told you that? Do you believe her?"

"She showed me old fashioned black-and-white photos of her and José from that time. There's one with them and Georgia O'Keefe, others with Ernest Blumenschein, Mabel Dodge Luhan, Betty Binkley, Ansel Adams... Daniel, it's amazing! Astra de la Luz is a living repository of art history!"

Daniel raised his eyebrows but still didn't react.

"Astra said that when she and José came to Earth, they had believed it would be very different from Tlaloc – *La Tierra* would be a place of beauty and hope."

Daniel was rarely bitchy, but he snorted. "If I can't say anything nice about something..."

I ignored him. "Astra and José thought that they would be safe here. Earth was the backwater of the galaxy. That's us, *corazón.* Anyway, their ideas about beauty and hope were dashed once they got here. All their information had come from the 19th Century! The limits on the speed of light and all that. What bitterness to arrive in the midst of the Great Depression, on the threshold of World War II! Anyway, like I said, they eventually settled here in Santa Fe, which was relatively calm. José, who we never met, took up sculpting – like you, Daniel! – and Astra took up painting – skills they already possessed as Tlalocean Judge-Priests."

"Did Astra talk about how they blended in with humans? Or what Tlaloceans look like?"

"Actually, at one point I asked Astra to show me her true appearance."

Daniel leaned forward. "Really? And did she?"

"Unfortunately, no. She said she couldn't spare the energy to do so. Astra was evasive but from the way she spoke I got the impression her race isn't all that different from humans. She said Tlaloceans have two

42

eyes, two arms, two legs, just like us."

Daniel didn't react. Instead he went over to the kiva, kneeled and started into the fire. "Is that all she said?"

"Well, Astra said that with effort they could pass for human – at least superficially. They had what Astra called "the power of transformation". Gifted Tlaloceans could basically rearrange their mass to transform into something else. Not immensely different, but enough to pass. And what they couldn't transform physically, they could make up for by using what she called "mind-craft." Like hypnosis, I guess."

Daniel looked up at me from the kiva. He seemed mildly amused and made a mesmerizing gesture with his fingers. "Roswell mind tricks."

"Not completely. The transformation was real. They became virtually human. But they could never completely erase Tlaloc. To do so would destroy the source of their power. That would kill them. So, mind-craft was necessary to help them fit in. Apparently, Tlaloceans are very gifted in all things involving transformations of matter and perceptions of the mind."

Daniel was staring into the kiva fire moodily. "Gifted" he repeated. "Imagine the gift of being able to change your appearance at will. Who wouldn't want that?"

"Me, Daniel. You too, I imagine. Astra said that once they assumed a form they rarely changed it. It's not just about creating an illusion. It's about altering their very structure down to their cells. By way of analogy, she said it takes a relatively small amount of energy to destroy a rock. But imagine how much more energy it would take to put it back together again. Something about the laws of *entropía* -- entropy. *Corazón*, you know that physics isn't my strongest subject. But the bottom line is that the process of transforming more than once was too deeply exhausting. Painful. Potentially lethal. Apparently a transformation at that deep and complex a level drained them of essential energy -- it could easily stop a heart. So once the form was selected it was risky not to stay settled in it."

"To be almost human but never so in truth." Daniel stroked his chin. "And whatever this *gift* entails, it's clearly not permanent! Astra has aged since we moved here– well before she got sick!"

"Yes. But apparently Tlaloceans age more slowly than humans. They are as mortal as we are, as vulnerable. She said on average they live to be around 150 Earth years old, which is pretty old."

Daniel nodded but said nothing.

"Astra and José arrived here in the 1930s but were actually born on Tlaloc around Earth-year 1890. They aged slower for part of that time because of the near speed-of-light trip it took to get here." I contemplated the Spanish words *la velocidad de la luz* and wondered, *Was that how Astra chose her last name?"*

"Once they got here, they continued to age normally. But you're right, Daniel. She's aged fast since we moved here. The last fourteen years have been the worst for Astra."

"She went through terrible grief when she became a widow. Remember, Nicky? We moved here not long after that."

"Yes she did. We didn't know the half of it. I mean the horrible way her husband died."

Daniel looked up sharply. "What are you talking about, Nick? What did Astra say to you about José?"

"A few months – maybe a year – before we moved to Santa Fe, José had gone to Taos to set up at one of the exhibits where Astra's paintings were showing. At night, while driving back to Santa Fe on the High Road, a car smashed into him and pushed him off a cliff. His car crashed, caught on fire, exploded. His body was never recovered."

Daniel shook his head angrily. "A damned drunk driver."

"No," I corrected. "It was the Zolteots. Actually, Earth kapos taking orders from the Zolteots. The stolen car that hit Josée was going 70 miles per hour. They found it abandoned the next day in Albuquerque. When the accident happened, there were two men in the kapo car. Some guy who was camping nearby witnessed the whole thing. The son of a bitch behind the wheel was identified as one Severo Lopez. He was never found. There was a manhunt for him but he crossed the border into Mexico and disappeared. The other *hombre* in the car was never identified at all."

"Astra's been known to be wrong, Nicky. To sometimes even back-pedal a story. There's just no reason to think that it was anything other than some drunk driver who hit Jose's car, got scared and fled the scene."

"No, Daniel. There's more. After José's car went over the cliff it didn't burst into flames right away. The camper who witnessed the accident saw this Lopez guy exit his car, stand at the cliff's edge and then shoot into José's car with an incendiary gun – what Astra described as a Zolteot firegun. *That's* what caused José's car to explode."

Daniel folded his arms, stood up and just looked at me. After an awkward moment he announced that he needed the bathroom. I waited for him. When he came back all he said was "Poor José..." He paused. When he spoke again, he sounded like a little boy. "Astra had once told me that José was intentionally killed. Later, when I tried to get more information she told me she was mistaken – she was a widow because of a drunk driver."

"He was murdered, Daniel. The Zolteot equivalent of a mob hit. When she got the news, Astra was petrified. And furious. She couldn't even share the truth with the police. She grieved and grew bitter. She realized that the Zolteots were here. They had targeted Earth for their next desert planet. They had infiltrated our society. They had promised wealth and power to human traitors willing to betray Earth. And they had begun to ferret out and hunt Tlaloceans. They offered the kapos a special bounty on Judge-Priests. Tlaloceans were no longer safe on Earth."

"Nicky, what you're telling me is that Zolteots and their collaborators have been on Earth for the last 14 years."

"Wrong, Daniel. I'm telling you that they've been here for the last 66 years"

I'd never seen his eyes bug out before. "*Jesús Cristo*, what did you say?"

"After José's murder, Astra learned that thousands of Zolteots had begun arriving on Earth since 2000, but were mostly in places like New York, L.A., Moscow or London. Santa Fe was a backwater. That's why they had caught her off guard – until José. But after José died, she dug deep and discovered that they were everywhere. In government, law, the media, the internet. They came as the Trojan Horse to weaken our response to their planned invasion. And to kill any Tlaloceans who might try to interfere."

Daniel suddenly looked nauseous. "How much time did she say we have?"

"Astra says three weeks. Maybe four."

Daniel's hand was on his mouth. "I think I'm going to throw up." He ran to the bathroom for the second time in ten minutes. I heard him wretch. I hadn't expected him to be this affected by Astra's story. I mean at this point who could say whether it was even true or just the ramblings of a dying old lady? Then I remembered. That old lady possessed the power of telekinesis. And somehow I could still sense her hovering in my mind. There was no question. She had told the truth. I had to will myself to keep from shaking again.

After making sure Daniel was alright, I went to the kitchen and got him a glass of water. When he came back looking pale, I sat him down on the loveseat and said, "drink this, *corazón*." He drank gratefully. After a few minutes he asked, "What else?"

"What else? Astra *La Vengadora*, I guess. Astra The Avenger. With José dead, the Tlaloceans in mortal danger, and the people of Earth acting like damned fools, Astra dedicated herself to reestablishing justice."

"Did she seek help? Surely, she and José weren't the only Tlaloceans to refugee to Earth!"

"She said about a thousand Tlaloceans had arrived in the 1930s and 1940s but by 2053 the vast majority of them had died without ever being replaced. Something about our magnetic field made it hard for most of them to have children. But she did say that there were still a few Judge-Priests on Earth."

"How many?"

"She wouldn't say. But the impression she gave me was that it was a pretty small number. Her first priority when she discovered the Zolteot threat was to reestablish contact with these Judge-Priests. This all happened shortly before we moved here."

"So, what happened? Did she create a team of vigilante justice warriors?"

"No. Everyone was too spread out. And most of the underground Tlalocean community had their own problems. There was no realistic way to pool resources except in the most dire circumstances."

"Meaning what?"

"Meaning a one-time pooling of power from across the Earth. They could channel that collective strength only once because it would drain most of them of their energies. And their lives."

"Is that where we're at now? The most dire of circumstances?"

I nodded and closed my eyes.

"Yes, Daniel. That's why Astra said before the cancer takes her, she must finish her painting – *La Pintura Grande*. She said it would be Earth's only defense. When it's done some time tonight she will use her mind to summon the surviving Judge-Priests to enter judgment on this painting – she called the process *La Manifestación*. She said most of the Judge-Priests are so old that manifesting the painting will unquestionably kill them – but they've been waiting for this day. They're ready to die and would rather perish fighting the Zolteots than in any other way."

Daniel rubbed his head and began pacing. "I understand," he said. The rain on the roof grew stronger. "Did Astra explain how her painting will save Earth?"

I threw my hands up in the air. "A leap of faith, Daniel. What other weapons have we got? The Zolteots are in every branch of government, every space agency, every army..."

Daniel repeated the words "leap of faith." He looked worried but seemed calmer than he was a few minutes earlier. "*Guapo*, do you understand what she meant by all of this concerning paintings and judgments and ... *La Manifestación?*"

"It's so simple, Daniel. And terrifying! Astra said there was power in art. That Judge-Priests had the power to create reality based on what they painted. *La Manifestación!* She said with all of the evil surrounding her – with the coming of the Zolteots, with the corruption of Earth's people – it was time to reshape reality. It was time to become *La Pintora* – the Painter. And, more often than not, that also meant becoming *La Vengadora*, the Angel of Vengeance."

Daniel looked away. "So Astra, *La Vengadora*, killed Zolteots? Vigilante retribution for José's murder?"

"She said her art could no longer directly affect the Zolteots – they had learned how to be immune to its effects 150 years ago, when they tried to take Tlaloc. But she said her art could certainly target kapos and otherwise affect humans and objects. When you talk about retribution...she did ultimately get her revenge. Severo Lopez—that kapo who killed José and fled to Mexico...? They found him hanging from a noose from a bridge in Juarez. His neck was broken."

"He committed suicide. A coincidence, I'm sure."

I looked at him and realized that, *brillante* as he may be, there's so much that Daniel didn't see.

"Daniel, did you know that Astra's house has a cellar?"

Daniel didn't respond directly. "I've seen a door and some steps. Astra said that she kept her painting supplies down there."

"She sent me down there this afternoon. You know what I saw? Paintings. Hundreds of them. Paintings that she's worked on in the years since José was killed. She's never even tried to exhibit most of them."

"Why are you telling me this?"

"In Astra's cellar, there's a painting of a man on a bridge. A man hanging from a noose. You can see from the angle that his neck is broken. The title of the painting is *La Ejecución de Severo Lopez*—The Execution of Severo Lopez.

Daniel licked his lips as if his mouth was too dry.

"When I came up from the cellar after looking at all those paintings, do you know what Astra said to me? '*Mijo*, she whispered, "Most artists make art to imitate life. But I make life imitate art!'"

I watched Daniel as he glanced up at some of the artworks in our living room. A wall-sculpture he had crafted out of bronze. Photographs from our wedding in San Francisco. And, finally, a portrait of Daniel, Ariel and me having a picnic on the grass at Marcy Park—an anniversary gift that we had received from the accomplished Santa Fe artist, Astra de la Luz.

Daniel sighed. "What if Astra painted that man *after* she learned of his suicide?"

"No, Daniel. Astra makes things happen! ¡La Manifestación! She uses her power as a Judge-Priest to *create* the reality she wants. You remember when her painting, *El Milagro*, was in the paper?"

Daniel looked uncomfortable. "I remember. That poor teenage girl who was paralyzed from a fall in the mountains. She broke her neck, but somehow had a miracle cure. Astra's painting showed her walking up the stairs onto the stage to receive her high school diploma. It was a beautiful story. Astra painted it nicely."

"Daniel. Astra didn't paint *El Milagro* to honor the crippled girl. Astra painted the crippled girl *into* health so she could have a miracle and graduate!"

Daniel's smile faded. He looked at me as if weighing what to say. Finally, he said, "That's quite a gift."

I whispered as if Astra were present and eavesdropping. "It's a terrifying gift. My God, Astra has the power to kill. And she has the power to heal."

Daniel was staring at me. I could see him trembling slightly. "A powerful gift indeed. And what gives her the right...?" He did not finish his sentence but just kept looking at me. He looked scared and angry at the same time.

"Daniel, you know what's really terrifying? The number of lives that Astra has affected, the way that *La Vengadora* has interfered with people's destinies."

Daniel stood up, walked over to the kiva and knelt facing the fire. "Even if what you say is true, I do not approve. Saving Earth from Zolteots is one thing. But, *Dios mío*, to assume the role of judge and executioner for all of mankind...? What gives her the right? Someone says *buenos días* the wrong way, she paints them into jail? Some critic hates her paintings? He ends up sweeping floors? *Híjole!* Arrogant, arrogant Astra."

"Why don't you tell me how you really feel about this, *corazón*?"

"Sorry, *guapo*. I just...Why don't you go on? What else did you see in the basement?"

"Well, there was a painting called *La Desgracia del Senador* – The Senator Disgraced."

Daniel nodded slowly. "Astra hated that man."

"Yes. And how easy for *La Vengadora* to remove him. Astra painted him discovered in bed with his lawyer's wife. And so the photographers found him. And within the week he was forced to resign."

Daniel was still pale and his voice had become flat. "I remember a painting she called *El Accidente*..."

"Those people had robbed three convenience stores and shot two people. She wanted them stopped before they robbed a fourth."

"I remember a painting called *El Jardín*..."

"Haven't you wondered how an old woman could grow maples and jacaranda trees and bougainvillea... in New Mexico?"

After a minute or so Daniel rubbed his neck and said, "I don't know how to react to this, Nicky. Awesome power in the hands of someone as vindictive as Astra...? Someone whose wisdom has faded? I love her, Nicky. But I stand by what I said. I do not approve."

"Well," I said honestly. "I love her too, but Astra scares the hell out of me."

51

Quietly he said, "Astra, Astra."

As the fire in the kiva went out, I felt released somehow. My job as Astra's go-between was done. Everything she had wanted me to say had been said.

Daniel put his hands over his face and then rubbed his eyes. "I'm really tired, *guapo.*"

"Me too." I made sure there were no hot embers in the kiva. Then I stood up listening to the rain on the roof. "Did you hear the thunder? The rain's getting stronger."

Daniel glanced at the window and yawned. "Let's finish talking in the morning. It's really late."

We let Ariel out. Then we turned out the lights and went to the bedroom. After I stripped down to my undershorts and brushed my teeth I found Daniel sitting up in bed waiting for me with an intense gaze in his eyes. Was he serious?

"Daniel, I don't think it's going to be that kind of night."

Tired as he was, he half-smiled. "I wasn't planning on that kind of night either, *guapo.* I just like looking at you. *Y, también....* I'm sad and worried. More tired than you can imagine."

I climbed into bed next to him and planted a kiss on his neck. His lips found mine... but just for a moment. Then he laid his head back on his pillow and sighed. "What an awful day," he said.

I put my hand on his chest and lightly brushed one of his nipples. Not to excite him. Just boy- play. He said "hm" and gently pushed my hand away.

I understood. "When the dust settles, Daniel. When this is over." He patted my arm lightly and then turned out the light.

Then, just as I was starting to fall asleep, Daniel started talking again. "Nicky, did Astra paint any self-portraits? Maybe showing her well again? Maybe vanquishing the cancer?"

I was sorry to dash that hope. No, *corazón*. She said something about not misusing the gift. You can't use it just for your own benefit. Otherwise, *La Manifestación* fails." I almost fell asleep again.

Then I remembered. "Daniel... I forgot. The last painting she allowed me to see was one she did yesterday. It was a portrait. Of her and José."

Daniel immediately turned his lamp back on.

He looked shocked. "What does that mean? Is she trying to bring José back from the dead?"

"No, Daniel. She wouldn't explain exactly, but I think it was the opposite. This painting, *Reunido*—was about reuniting with José after she dies. She was very proud of it. She said it would be second in her heart only to that other painting she said she's kept for you in her closet.

Daniel leaned an arm on his pillow and looked at me. "Tell me about this painting of José and Astra."

I had seen so many paintings that afternoon but this one stood out. "Astra and José, they both look old – but healthy-old, you understand?" Daniel nodded. "They're holding hands and sort of float-walking towards something bright and full of color. Tlaloc maybe. Heaven. Who knows? But that's the future she was creating for herself for... after tonight." I sighed. "I have to say, *corazón*... It was stunning. Magical. One of her best."

"Did she happen to say who..."

"She said that she wanted us to have that painting."

For some reason my description of this painting moved him more than anything else I had said all evening. He surreptitiously wiped his eyes. Then he did so a second time and this time I sat up and held his head against my chest as he began to sob. I kissed his forehead. "*Mi corazón,"* I said stroking his hair. *"Mi amado corazón."*

A few minutes later when Daniel's tears had calmed down, he said "That painting sounds beautiful, Nicky. Truly. Maybe in the morning—."

At that moment we were startled by two simultaneous things. First, there was the loudest blast of thunder we had yet heard. Then there was a banging sound on the roof, like a bobcat or an owl had landed on it. We both looked at the ceiling and listened to whatever was on the roof slowly creep across it. Finally, whatever creature it was must have leaped into one of the aspen trees. The noise stopped. I was thoroughly weirded out. "What the hell was that?!" I exclaimed.

Daniel seemed numb rather than anxious. He got out of bed slowly, laboriously and put his hand on the windowpane looking out at the mist. I asked him what was wrong. I had to ask a second time. He didn't turn around. "Astra is dead," he said painfully.

"Are you sure?" He didn't respond. There was nothing to say. Of course he was sure. Daniel's intuition about such things was remarkable. His heightened sensitivity is one of the gifts that make him a truly great artist.

I haven't been a very good Catholic since leaving SoCal, but I got out of bed, crossed myself and stood with him at the window looking out at the late October rain. We entwined fingers. I still remembered my Latin and spoke the words *"Requiem aeternum, dona eis domine."* To my surprise, Daniel joined me when we got to *"et lux perpetua luceat ei, requiescat in pace."*

Those are the words we said. But did I mean them? After everything this old woman had told me... Look. Astra had been my friend. She was a great artist with a long, fascinating life. But she was also *La Vengadora,* the avenging angel who had appointed herself judge and executioner of so many. True, she had helped many people, but she was far from innocent. She was a bitter Tlalocean Judge-Priest who had caused much death. And she had helped to destroy her own planet.

Did Astra de la Luz deserve eternal peace?

We got back in bed and turned out the lights. Daniel lay facing the window. I spooned him tightly with my right hand around his waist. I whispered "I love you, Daniel." He took my hand, kissed it and put it back on his belly. I held him this way, listening to the sound of rain on the roof until I finally fell into a fitful sleep.

PART III: THE SCULPTOR

*J*esús *Cristo*! I don't want to scare you but a bolt of lightning just struck maybe two blocks away from here! The thunder was like a cannon! Ariel's hiding under the bed. I myself keep wavering between panic and calm resolve. I need to write. *Ay*, I need the clarity. Oh journal, help me stay sane in this insane time! Help me to keep going!

Alright. Saturday morning, October 31, 2066. I got up first and made coffee. When I saw Daniel zombie-walk into the kitchen I almost dropped the coffee pot. He looked just awful! His face was unusually drawn and there were dark circles under his eyes. He said he'd had a bad night—a night of grief and war-dreams. Clearly.

We let Ariel out in the rain. At least the air was fresh and clean. Everything glistened. Once Ariel came back in, Daniel and I had our coffee and toast in silence. I've never seen him so jittery and distracted. He didn't check email, ignored the news. At one point I saw him just staring at the wall. I finally tapped on the shoulder. "Corazón," I said. "We can't put this off any longer. Let's get ready and go over there."

He looked at me blankly, then nodded once. Softly, he said, "*Sí, Nicky. ¿Como no?*"

I drove us in his car to the Galleria Astra. My own car was still parked there under Astra's alder tree.

We knocked on the heavy oak door. When there was no answer, I used the key I had kept from yesterday. Astra had said I would need it.

We walked into the gallery. It smelled musty and there was a slight echo. No one was there and it still felt like a haunted museum. Daniel called out Astra's name but... nothing. We knew why, of course. Then we walked into the old part of the house where the original pine floor creaked. I stopped in the parlor briefly to look at the faded sofa where Astra had sat yesterday afternoon. The terror I felt when Astra had used her mind to control my body and move furniture still made my pulse race. But now everything looked tidy and quiet and sad.

My breathing got shallow as we approached the bedroom. *Stay calm,* I told myself. The door was closed. We knocked. No one answered.

Daniel took my arm. "Nicky, would you mind if I go in first? Alone?"

I understood. "Of course."

Daniel entered the bedroom and closed the door before I could peek in. I heard a noise that sounded like muffled sobbing for three or four minutes. Then silence. After another minute or two, I knocked. Daniel said for me to come in.

When I walked into the bedroom, he had already covered Astra with the blanket so that I couldn't see her dead body. I knew she was gone because her bifocals were on the nightstand. I had never before seen them off her face.

Daniel was kneeling beside the bed. His cheeks were wet. I turned away as he whispered something to the blanketed body. I wanted him to have his private moment.

"I'd like to say good-bye too, Daniel."

"You got to see her alive yesterday, *corazón.* Please don't ask me to remove the blanket."

I processed this. I was very uncomfortable being in the room with Astra's corpse. "Maybe we should call Santa Fe County and then leave."

"Not possible, Nicky. There can be no coroner. Can you imagine the questions? What if they want to do an autopsy?" I nodded understanding. "Nicky, didn't you say Astra gave you a phone number?"

Of course! I remembered the notepaper with the phone number for Hectór, the man she had directed me to. It was in my wallet.

"Who do you think this Hectór is?" he asked.

"One of the few that are left, I would guess."

Daniel said, "Let me have the number. I'll call him in a few minutes." I handed him the notepaper. I watched him study it, then put it in his own wallet.

"Daniel, what are we..."

He cut me off. "Nicky, we need to look at the painting."

We left the bedroom and walked into the studio. The easel was right where I had last seen it, in the middle of the room. A canvas rested on the easel and, as yesterday, the canvas was hidden by a drop cloth. Astra's brushes and palette were still on the little table next to her empty chair.

We walked around to the front of the covered canvas. Daniel took hold of my right hand with his left. He said "Ready?" I answered "ready." Then he pulled off the drop cloth.

We looked at Astra's last work, her *Pintura Grande*. But it was so simple! Almost childish! What had taken her so long to paint it? At first, I didn't understand what I was seeing. It was obviously a scene in space. An illustration for science fiction perhaps? What I saw was a beautiful, sparkling planet – almost completely dominated by a dozen shades of blue with some white at the poles and just a few hints of land here and there – islands notable for their blank lack of features in a vast world-sized sea. The painting was titled *El Nuevo Mundo*–the New World.

I turned to Daniel, "I don't understand. Is that Tlaloc?"

Daniel fell on his knees and moaned.

"What? Daniel, what is it?"

He didn't hear me. He moaned, "No! *Dios mío*, no!"

"Daniel, what did she do?" I got louder and more insistent. "What did Astra do?"

He looked up at me from the floor. His eyes were wet and a little yellow–jaundiced from worry and lack of sleep. Never have I seen Daniel so stricken.

I tried to speak calmly but my voice shook. "Daniel–*corazón*–" I knelt next to him and put my hand on his shoulder. I whispered. "What did Astra do?"

He reached his hand out to touch the painting but then recoiled. Then he whispered the words I had quoted last night about the Zolteots. "Water was poison to them..."

It took me a second. Then I gasped and started to lose control of my breathing.

He pointed to a cratered white circle in the distance. He couldn't speak. He didn't need to. It was a moon. Not just any moon. There was Tycho. And Copernicus. It was *our* Moon.

I jumped up in shock! This almost entirely blue orb was our own planet under water!

Astra had both loved *La Tierra* and hated it. Deep in her heart was a desire to punish the people of Earth for their perfidy. Even deeper in her heart was hatred for the Zolteots. She had decided to sink the ship to deprive the pirates of their prize. Astra's last judgment was that Earth, like Tlaloc before us, must drown.

And, if her story from yesterday was to be believed, behind that judgment was the power of almost every geriatric Tlalocean Judge-Priest who had refugeed to Earth, most of whom would now be dead

60

from the final exertion of manifesting this painting. Except, maybe, this Hectór. And if Hectór lived, maybe there were others? Judge-Priests who could perhaps reverse Astra's judgment...?

I was grasping at straws. The handful of Tlaloceans still alive would be too weak to save Earth. What was the power of the few against the judgment of Astra and her secret cabal of Judge-Priests?

I fell back onto the floor next to Daniel staring at this painting, knowing that whatever Astra had painted would come true. Randomly I thought of the Robert Frost poem. *Some say the world will end in fire, Some say in ice.* I closed my eyes and thought, *wrong on both counts.*

Suddenly I was consumed with fury. Out loud I said "Astra, how dare you?! How *dare* you?! ¡Bruja! You witch!"

I scared Daniel. He tried to calm me down. He tried to hold me, but I threw him off. I had begun to lose my mind.

"Oh my God, Daniel! It can't be! She didn't have the power to destroy Earth. Did she?"

"Nick, *entiendes...* we don't know anything about her contacts with other Tlaloceans She kept a lot of secrets."

I began to weep. "Oh my God, we're going to die!"

Daniel grabbed me and held me in his arms. "No, Nicky. No! That much I know. You and I will live. That's one thing you will never need to worry about!"

"What are you saying?! The world is coming to an end!" I looked out the window at the rain. How stupid I was to have thought that the air smelled fresh and that rain was a good thing!

Astra! I spat on the window cursing her. Then I collapsed on the floor. Daniel tried to comfort me, but I wouldn't let him touch me.

Daniel sighed and walked into the parlor deep in thought, slowly looking at the various artworks on the wall. After a while I got up. I didn't want to be alone. I followed him and watched him look at Astra's *retablos*, a wrought-iron sculpture, two old 19th Century portraits and, by the kiva, an 18th Century altarpiece that was her most prized possession. On the coffee table was a bust of Astra which I recognized. It had been sculpted by Daniel.

When Daniel saw that I was watching him he hesitated and then came to me. He put his hand on my shoulder. Very gravely, he said "There's nothing we can do, Nicky. *Nada*. Maybe it's true that the world is coming to an end." He paused. Then in a firm voice he added, "... but not for us. You and I are safe."

I was exhausted and numb. "What do you mean?"

A pause. A long pause. "No more secrets," he muttered.

"Daniel, what are you talking about? What secrets?"

"Look into my eyes, Nicky." I did. These were the eyes of my beloved... except that as I stared into them, I saw that the amber flecks in his eyes seemed to grow bigger and the brown parts seemed to diminish. My mouth opened but for a moment I couldn't say anything.

Then I found my voice. "How are you doing that?"

Then Daniel took my hand and locked fingers with me. He said "Nothing ends for us. Astra made sure of that."

"Daniel, what could Astra possibly...?"

Silently, he took my hand and led me back into Astra's bedroom. Ignoring the covered body, he opened her clothes closet and, after fumbling for a moment, retrieved an oil painting. He propped it against the foot of Astra's deathbed. I gasped when I saw it. It was a portrait of Daniel and me. We were in this very house. I had never seen this painting before. It didn't look like any of her newer paintings and was unlike any picture of me I had ever seen. It was clearly me, but I looked like my grandfather! I was wrinkled and balding. Involuntarily, I reached up

62

and touched my head to make sure I still had all my hair. My eyes were rheumy and heavy. I looked at Daniel's image – he looked mature, with white in his temples and a rather dashing grey mustache. He didn't look as old as I did. But his eyes... what happened to his eyes? The painting was titled *Los Hijos*.

I turned to Daniel. "'The Sons'? I don't understand..."

Grabbing *Los Hijos*, Daniel led me from the bedroom and back into the parlor. He propped the painting on a chair so we could look at it as we spoke. "Please don't be upset, Nicky. A long time ago I asked Astra for this. I asked her... for you."

"For me? What are you talking about?"

"After I met you at my opening in San Francisco thirteen years ago... after we had dated for a few weeks. I wanted you... very badly. In fact, I'd never wanted a man the way I wanted you. Not just as a lover but as a true partner. I had to have you. But I had sworn off painting. It was a cheat, you see. And yet... Nicholas, my husband... I couldn't imagine life without you. So, I sent your photo to Astra. I asked her to paint us together as we are in this painting. She did that just a few months before we moved to Santa Fe."

I could only look at him with dumb incomprehension.

Daniel cleared his throat. "As a matter of fact, Astra *caused* us to come to Santa Fe. It was soon after José was killed. She painted us here, in this picture, so that you and I would be together and safe in this house for a long, long time."

I picked my jaw up off the floor. "Wait a minute, Daniel. You knew Astra back in..."

He paused and swallowed.

"Nicky... Astra was my mother. I couldn't tell you before because ... well, because it's not our way."

I stared at him for ten seconds. *Our* way. The Tlalocean way. A terrifying comprehension dawned on me. How could I be so blind! I drew back in horror and began to back out of the room.

Daniel followed me into the gallery saying "Nicky, wait!"

I was terrified of him but furious as well. I turned on him. "Daniel Vigil Cruz, you son-of-a-bitch! I can't speak. I can't even breathe! Are you saying what I think you're saying? You're a... lie? An alien? You're not human?!" My mouth continued to move but only made sputtering sounds. I felt like passing out. He tried to touch me and I hissed at him like a snake. "Get away from me!"

His hand covered his mouth as if he were trying to take back his bizarre disclosure. "Dammit, Nicky. Give me a chance!"

I collapsed sobbing on the gallery floor surrounded by Astra's paintings. "A chance for what? What in hell *are* you? What do you want from me?!"

"Stand up, Nicky. Let's talk. Face to face." He held out his hand. I was scared, but after a moment I took it.

He led me to the dining room. We sat on old chairs with the dining table as a buffer between us. Then he gazed into my eyes. "Look at me, Nicky. See me as I really am." The amber-yellow glow in his eyes grew in intensity and began to radiate light. My eyes grew big with fear. This is what I thought I had wanted Astra to show me the day before - but that had been more a bluff than a true desire to know. I never truly believed she wasn't human. But now Daniel was trying to show me how wrong I had been. *Dios*, I was not ready for this. I fled the table, ran back into the parlor and tried to hide next to the kiva like a child. I knew he wasn't trying to scare me, but I couldn't be in the same room with him. That Astra had lied to me all of the years I had known her could be forgiven. She had been a friend - a peevish friend - but nothing more. But my own husband? The man I had devoted my very life to? If he wasn't human, what in hell was he?! My God, everything I knew and cared about from the survival of Earth to the survival of my marriage was suddenly unraveling.

Daniel's eyes normal again, he followed me into the parlor and stood in the doorway so I couldn't escape. Then he advanced towards me – not threatening but very determined. I stood up and grabbed the poker which was placed next to the kiva.

"Nicky, what on Earth do you think you're doing?"

I brandished the poker. "Don't come any closer, Daniel."

He didn't stop advancing. When he had me cornered, he grabbed my arm, pried the poker out of my hand and threw it on the floor. I was shaking as he took hold of my hand. I growled and yanked it back. He grabbed my hand again more forcefully and then dragged me to the sofa where I had sat with Astra the day before. He forced me to sit.

"You're going to listen to me, Nicky. You're going to hear me out. We've been together for thirteen years, Goddammit, and you married me, and you're going to give me a chance!"

"I can't deal with this," I moaned. "I just can't." I started to get up to leave.

Daniel pointed back at the sofa, silently demanding–and begging—for me to sit.

I waited for the sound of the doors to lock as they had yesterday when Astra imprisoned me with telekinesis and controlled my mind. But it didn't happen this time. As I waited, it dawned on me that if he were truly Astra's son, Daniel could have used his mind to control me. And yet he had chosen not to. Maybe I should hear Daniel out. Why was I willing to give Astra the benefit of the doubt but not her son–the man who happened to be my husband?

Slowly I sank back onto the sofa. When Daniel saw that I was willing to listen he nodded to me very gravely. He spoke quietly, "Thank you, *corazón*."

"What now?" I said dully.

He didn't answer right away. He seemed to be weighing how to tell me his truth.

"Daniel...?

He made his decision and exhaled loudly. "Now? Now I show you the truth. If you're ready."

I nodded warily. Daniel took my trembling hand and kissed it like the romantic gentleman he has always been. His hands shook. Why he was as frightened as I was! "Are you ready, Nicky?"

I nodded curtly. "I'm ready."

Daniel took a deep breath, backed away and stood facing me from in front of Astra's kiva. To my surprise, he began to unbutton his shirt. After removing his topshirt, he pulled his undershirt over his head. He now stood before me exposing the flesh of his bare torso. "Do you see me?" he said. "Do you see the truth?"

What truth? I was puzzled. But he was not done. I watched him take off his shoes. Then, when I saw that Daniel intended to remove his trousers, I said "Daniel, you don't need to do this." He said, "Nicky, you deserve the truth of who I am." Then he removed his trousers, his socks, finally his undershorts. Daniel now stood before me in Astra's living room completely nude. He held both arms out to his side like da Vinci's *Vitruvian Man*. "Now do you see me? Now do you see the truth?"

Why was he asking this? He looked perfect, like one of his marble statues, like *El Hombre Que Canta* from all those years ago. Improbable as it sounds, even though he was older, he looked even better now. He was, to my eyes, a uniquely sexy Latino man with a handsome face and bronze skin - well-muscled, smooth, narrow in the hips, nicely endowed and completely human. By any standard, he was a paragon of masculine beauty. An ancient Greek Adonis. Michelangelo's David. How many times had I intimately explored and tasted of that trembling flesh?

The very thought made me question if I was going mad. Under these most dire of circumstances, I once again had to fight for control of my own body. But this time it wasn't an alien mind that was controlling me. It was desire. I had to catch my breath, ignore the blood rushing to my groin and pretend that Daniel's naked body didn't arouse me. Maybe he wasn't human but his very beauty filled my senses.

If Daniel was aware of the animal effect, he had on me he didn't show it. He had a disclosure to make. His eyes burned into mine as I remained frozen on the sofa. Then he gestured with his fingers and said, "Come here, Nicky..." When I hesitated he said, "*Por favor*. I promise I won't seduce you."

I still couldn't figure out what this was about. Transfixed, I rose and walked slowly up to him. We stood face to face, me fully clothed before this perfect nude statue of a man who I thought I had known. He said "give me your hand."

I hesitated and then complied. He took my hand and placed it over his heart. Instead of the normal beat I felt his heart pounding in triplets. I gasped and pulled my hand back but he firmly put it back on his chest. "I'm sorry to have hidden this from you, *guapo*. On Tlaloc we have six chambers to our heart. I mask it with a simple touch of my hand to your mind." His hand touched my head, lightly brushing my hair and giving me gooseflesh. "It's not hard to influence people's thoughts," he said. "Or their perceptions."

I again pulled my hand back, unable to grasp what he was saying. I started to turn away but Daniel said not to—that I had nothing to fear.

"Nicky, give me your hand again."

His voice was changing, growing deeper somehow. It developed a rumbling undertone which was not human but hinted at a reptilian growl. Then, as I looked up at his face, I could see its structure change right before my eyes. My jaw dropped and the erection I had been consciously fighting instantly vanished as eroticism transformed into horror right before my eyes. I was too shocked to move! Daniel's eyes became pure fire. His hair receded into a yellow-green scaly baldness. And the hand holding mine was now leather rough and had an extra digit.

I was frozen with fear. I almost screamed but Daniel was speaking softly - words I didn't understand - and somehow Daniel's Tlalocean murmurings crept into my mind and kept me from panicking. After a few moments, with his six-fingered hand Daniel guided my trembling hand across his chest. I had stroked that smooth chest a thousand times. But this time, under the skin I felt... scales. I recoiled but he grabbed my hand back. "Again," he said. Now when he placed it on his chest the skin was completely gone. I felt only leathery scales. Both terrified and fascinated, I moved my hand from his chest down to his stomach. Then I ran my right hand across his left hip and down the thigh. Finally, I reached for where his manhood protruded, but it was gone!–fully retreated into his torso. Everywhere that I touched, his smooth, bronze skin disappeared into reptile scales.

Daniel's Tlalocean murmurings stopped. Nausea hit me hard. I stumbled and fell back. I landed on the sofa willing myself not to throw up and forced my eyes closed. Daniel stood as still as a statue, neither moving nor speaking, as he waited patiently for me to process what my eyes had seen. After half a minute I opened my eyes and finally looked at what he had never before wanted me to see. Daniel was not human – not even close. The height and weight were about the same, but he

68

was a scaly creature, iridescent green and yellow, with a lizard mouth and eyes of fire. There was nothing human about him. Daniel was a monster. An alien creature from Tlaloc.

I ran to Astra's toilet, projectile vomited and then guzzled two glasses of water while I stared into the mirror. Over and over I whispered to myself *what do I do?, what do I do?*

A deep lizard voice from the parlor answered the question the Daniel-creature could not possibly have heard. It rumbled, "You come back here. We finish this."

I took a deep breath and crept back into the parlor slowly, warily. I held back the urge to vomit again. The Daniel-creature was still there in front of the kiva. Two eyes, two arms, two legs, just like Astra had said. Yes, she had told the truth about Tlaloceans. But she had left out everything that mattered!

In that deepened voice with growling undertones it said, "Nicholas Clements, man of Earth... Now do you see me? Now do you see the truth?"

"¡Basta!" I said. "Enough! I see you!"

Then the thing that was Daniel waved its lizard hand in the air and my nausea evaporated. Gradually, the reptile in him disappeared, once again invisible below his skin. Within two or three minutes of metamorphosis Daniel again displayed human flesh. He was once again muscled and exceptionally handsome. But I knew now that this was merely a mask. How could he ever be beautiful again?

Understand something. Daniel's beauty was something I appreciated. How I loved to look at him, to touch that smooth skin, those defined muscles. But his beauty was never why I loved him. I loved him because of his talent, because of his character. That he aroused me was because of who he was inside. I had always prided myself on being open-minded. On not caring that much about appearances. But when I looked at Daniel now, all I could see were scales and lies and I couldn't say which one terrified me more. I stared without speaking for at least a minute. I was paralyzed. What could I possibly say?

"Nicky..." he said quietly.

The sound of Daniel's normal voice after putting me through this horrific display almost killed me right then and there.

"Daniel, why did you lie to me?" I moaned. "In the name of God, what *are* you?"

Now it was Daniel who couldn't speak. He just stood there gazing at me for a long time—as if he were looking into my soul. Finally, he shrugged and very simply said, "I'm just me, *guapo*. Your husband." He saw my fear. He finally moved and approached me, the emotions displayed on his face as naked as his body. The skin, muscles, hair, navel, genitals, lips, eyes—every aspect of his human appearance seemed so real. And with that wounded expression on his face, he seemed more vulnerable than frightening. He had tears in his eyes. My own eyes watered in response. He said nothing. Instead, he pulled my head forward and we touched foreheads.

And then Daniel collapsed.

I yelled for help but there was no one to hear me. I felt for a pulse but couldn't find it. I cried out, "please, Jesus, don't let him die!" Then I put my ear to his chest and heard that strange heartbeat in triplets. He was breathing. It was shallow but – thank God – Daniel was alive.

Astra had warned me. This process of transformation, she had said, was "deeply exhausting. Painful. Possibly lethal." Daniel had shown me who he really was and it had badly hurt us both.

I tried to revive him, but he didn't react. He was shivering cold and his breath was erratic. I looked at him and saw neither scales nor skin

– only a being in need. I picked him up as if he were my child. To me he was not heavy. I carried him to Astra's sofa and sat back holding his suffering body cradled across my lap. There was a Navajo blanket within reach. I grabbed it and placed it over his shivering flesh. I closed my eyes, breathed deeply and wondered at the mystery of the classic Renaissance sculpture that our real life now modeled.

After a minute, Daniel inhaled a deep shuddering breath and opened his eyes. Weakly, he said, "Are you still here, *guapo?*"

"I'm here, *corazón,*" I answered.

He smiled gently, closed his eyes and made no effort to move. After another minute, in a haggard voice he said, "Now do you see the truth?"

I tried to hide that my cheeks were wet with tears. "Yes, *mijo.* Now I see the truth."

After a few more seconds, he opened his eyes and looked at me -- looked at me with such love. "I know how ugly I must seem to you. Don't worry. For you, Nicky – for us – this…" he smiled weakly and touched the human-looking flesh of his torso and face "… is what I am now. And will be until I die."

I was silent. This fragile, naked being trusted me utterly. Daniel had taken an irrevocable leap of faith and thrown himself on my mercy.

Mercy. The subject of judgment had become a sore one and my thoughts were a jumble. Should I hate Daniel because he was not truly human? Was it not natural to be repulsed? Should I give in to burning anger because he had misled me? And yet… I knew why he had lied. His survival had been at stake. And yet, who was this man? A vicious alien attacker? Some vile villain? No. A kind, gentle artist. And, now, an orphan. Should we not grieve together over Astra? Should I not join in his grief over a father who was killed by kapos conspiring with a supremely evil enemy? *Ay de mí,* could I pretend for one second that I

71

didn't respect the extraordinary courage Daniel has shown? Imagine! Living silently with the unimaginable loss of a homeworld and all that died with it: his people's culture, history, language And now he was in more danger than ever! Jesus Christ, to think of my Daniel slaughtered by the Zolteots destroys me! What do I do? *Dios mío*, what do I do?

I looked down. Daniel was breathing better. He was no longer shivering and had fallen asleep. I wanted to stroke his hair or kiss his forehead but held back. I couldn't get past the yellow and green scales, the lizard mouth, the eyes burning fire. And yet...was I supposed to think Daniel was in some way evil or unworthy? Could I believe for even one second that this strange alien being–this suffering *man* who had almost died for me–who I now cradled as if he were my own son–didn't love me? Could I pretend for even one second that I didn't love him?

As if he had read my mind, Daniel unexpectedly opened his eyes and looked deep into mine. "*Muchas gracias, guapo.*"

I sighed, not at all certain, and said "*De nada.*"

Daniel and I sat together this way – silently and without expectation – for probably ten more minutes. I felt his body grow warmer and his breath become regular. "Are you better?" I asked. He said yes, he was. Finally, I helped him sit up and pushed him away—but gently. "Get dressed, Daniel." He answered me with a soft, sad smile. "*Sí, guapo. ¿Como no?*"

One article at a time I watched him put his clothes back on, his underclothes, his designer jeans, his Armani shirt. He dressed like a normal man just as I've seen him dress on the 4400 mornings we've spent together. But he was *not* a normal man! His bizarre revelation had changed everything. Could I still love him? Impossible, no? He was a monster! On the other hand, doesn't everyone have a bit of monster inside them? Am I such a paragon of humanity? With the love Daniel has given me through the years, with the beauty he has given the world, could anyone fairly call him an abomination? He was a worthy, decent man.

But he was *not* a man! Maybe he could keep it closeted for awhile – maybe even for the rest of our lives together – but men do not have iridescent yellow and green scales, lizard tongues and fire-amber eyes. Maybe he could hypnotize me, but how long could that last? Worse, we'd be living a lie! Before I moved to San Francisco all those years ago, I'd had enough of living in a closet. Lorna Sanchez. My so-called parents who severed all ties with me simply because of who I am. Was this what I had given everything up for? Just to exchange one closet for another? I had a lot of thinking to do and a whole lot of questions. Where to start?

"How old are you, Daniel?"

"I was born in 1955. 111 years ago. Here in Santa Fe. I may be Tlalocean physically, but I've never seen Tlaloc. *Soy puro Nuevo México.* So, you see, *corazón,* I'm home. And our age difference doesn't have to matter. It's true that I'm much older than you. But the remainder of our lives should align perfectly. We'll grow old together. We'll probably die around the same time – many years from now."

Dios mío! My husband was 111 years old! He was born before my long-dead grandparents!

"Why didn't you ever tell me Astra was your mother?"

Daniel looked at me as if the answer was obvious. "We've been in *hiding,* Nicky. If one of us was discovered and killed, the other might still survive. And yet we also needed to be near each other. *La familia,* you see. Especially after the death of *mi padre.* I thought she was be-ing paranoid–maybe even demented–when she said that the Zolteots were coming. But I couldn't take the risk. I had to come back to Santa

Fe. But soon after *mi padre* died, she also told me that she had learned about two Tlaloceans who had been murdered, one in Los Angeles, one in Tokyo. Naturally, I wondered about my father also, but she swore to me that her original suspicions were wrong—that *mi padre* had died due to a drunk driver. So that's what I've believed all these years—until you told me the terrible truth last night. Either way, starting around 14 years ago—whether by coincidence or design—Tlaloceans were starting to turn up dead under suspicious circumstances. Then, when you and I were walking in the Castro right after we got engaged, I saw one. A Zolteot in San Francisco. Do you remember when I made us duck into a bar that one night because I said I was trying to avoid someone I used to know?"

I nodded numbly.

"That's when I realized that it was true. The Zolteots were here. I needed to be with Astra for her protection as well as my own. Nicky, I apologize for badly miscalculating. I thought we were at the earliest stages of an improbable Zolteot threat. If they were truly targeting Earth—and that was a big "if"—I thought it would not be until hundreds of years in the future—long after you and I are gone. Well, Astra was right, I was wrong. What's left of my people are in grave danger. As are yours. Except—for what it's worth—I'm convinced *mi madre's Pintura Grande* will force the Zolteots to abandon Earth."

"The information Astra asked me to give you yesterday. You already knew all along that there were Zolteots here? And yet you let me ramble on and on?"

"Hold on, Nicky. Seventy-five percent of what you told me yesterday was news to me – a complete shock, in fact. I had no idea that the Judge-Priests had voluntarily drowned Tlaloc, for instance. I mean– *¡Dios en el cielo!*– that blew me away. As for the Zolteots, Astra only told me half-truths. So how could I possibly know that an improbable Zolteot invasion of Earth was suddenly a certainty? And that it was weeks rather than centuries away? Astra wanted me close, she wanted me wary and alert to the Zolteot threat, but at the same time she was always lying to me, manipulating me, trying to protect me. I had seen Zolteots with my own eyes but had no idea how threatening their numbers actually were. I was misled again and again! Astra swore to me that *mi padre* was killed by a drunk driver. Dammit, look at the way I had to find out that *mi amado padre* was murdered!" Daniel banged his fist on the table in frustration."

I listened silently astounded that Tlalocean family dynamics born of a planet light years away could keep pace with those of Earth for sheer dysfunction.

"Nicky, you knew my mother—in some ways better than I did. You know how cunning she was. Always scheming, always calculating." At that moment Daniel's face relaxed and he grew thoughtful. "Ay, but she loved me. I know that she did what she felt she had to do. Mostly she was worried about our survival—especially now that an Earth human—you, *mi amado esposo*—was part of the picture. But, Nicky, don't assume that I know more than I do! Do you realize as we sit here today, I don't know even one single Tlalocean, let alone any Judge-Priests? Astra told you to give me this phone number for Hectór, but *¿quién es él?* Who the hell is he to me? Tlalocean minds are not linked telepathically, Nicky. They can be, but Tlaloceans *insist* upon their privacy. An instinctive loathing for social contact rests deep in the Tlalocean soul. Haven't you ever wondered why I was never interested in making friends? Why I hated exhibition openings as well as that whole San Francisco high life of shallow hangers-on and predators? I hated it! You and Ariel are all I want in this life. I am a lone wolf by nature."

"Well, you certainly put on a good act, Daniel. You've always seemed like a popular, suave, self-assured *hombre*."

Daniel responded drily. "I'm a good actor, Nicky. It's one of my gifts."

"One of your gifts," I said mockingly. "So, lone wolf, here's my question. How do I forgive you? Or trust anything you say? You've just admitted that you're a liar and an actor. I'm not some art patron or critic for you to manipulate. I'm your husband. I've trusted you body and soul, yet you've kept every aspect of your identity secret from me! Every single day since I met you. Thirteen years of lies!"

"Yes," he said quietly. "I've lied. About everything except who I am inside and what I feel. Doesn't that count?"

"I don't know, Daniel. Does it?"

He began to pace. My bitter words clearly tortured him. Finally, Daniel came over to me. Instead of sitting next to me as an equal, he kneeled in front of me like a beggar. He didn't touch me, but gazed up into my eyes and spoke very gently. "I'm sorry. Please forgive me, Nicky. I can never make up for the lies I've told you. But there were reasons for them which I'd like you to understand. It was Astra...*mi madre* who begged me to keep my identity secret. She *begged* me, Nicky. On her knees, pleading, just the way I'm on my knees before you now. Can't you understand? My mother wanted this for my protection. You see, if push ever came to shove, she didn't want the Zolteots to figure out that I was her son." He hesitated and then locked eyes with me. "And she didn't want the Zolteots to discover that I was destined to be Tlaloc's last surviving Judge-Priest."

I gasped slightly. The last surviving–*Oh, Daniel!* His importance to his people had not occurred to me. The sadness made me ache.

"Astra was not only a Judge-Priest, Nicky. She was a mother. It tortured her to know that her only son was a lonely outsider on a strange planet, probably the last of his kind. *Mi madre* desperately wanted me to have a chance at happiness. That could only happen if my true identity remained a secret. She and my father had previously convinced me to change my last name and to pursue my artistic education and experience away from here, to go to New York, to México. They wanted me to forge my own identity.

"Then *mi padre* died and my mother fell into a deep depression. But her will to live returned– in part because of you, Nicky! How she rejoiced when I told her about you. How she wept for joy when you and I got married! Later, when you and I moved to Santa Fe and bought the gallery next to hers, our presence energized her and eased her grief–and her anxiety–over *mi padre's* death. But can you imagine what torture it was for her to see me and yet not be able to embrace me as her son? You see, the fear consumed her day and night that she might expose me. That at any moment the Zolteots might find and murder me. Nicky, it was very hard for her to look at *you* and not embrace you as her son-in-law. She adored you and trusted you more than you can ever know. She wanted to be sure you were never endangered because of your status as my consort. *Corazón*, I'm so sorry about the lies. They hurt us all. But please know that they kept us alive."

I tried not to shed tears but couldn't help it. I remembered how truly Astra had been my friend. I remembered listening to Daniel weep quietly at night with some private sorrow when he thought I was asleep. I began to cry openly listening to the sound of the rain softly drizzling on Astra's roof.

Daniel, his own eyes moist, was hesitant to touch me. It took a few minutes before I could speak again. Finally, I said "Why me? Why an Earth human?"

This time Daniel was not shy and put his very human hand on

my arm. "Nicky, it hardly mattered that there were no Tlaloceans who made it to Earth who were the right age, or sex, or caste. There was you. I was drawn to you the minute I met you." He put his right hand firmly on my thigh as the other hand creeped into the small of my back. "More than drawn. Powerfully attracted like nothing I've ever experienced."

I sighed deeply. Lord knows, I've felt that same almost preternatural attraction. But at that particular moment the touch of his alien hands made me very uncomfortable. I got up, walked a few feet away and then faced him. I could see that my tacit rejection of him physically hurt his feelings. Too bad. "How can I ever know if I really love you, Daniel? Or if I'm just a slave to Astra's painting of us?"

Daniel stared at me for a second. Then the nature of my problem finally dawned on him. "You have it wrong, Nicky! Tlalocean paintings can't control the heart! *Mi madre's* painting is not a love potion or some supernatural contract yoking us together! *Los Hijos* is not a judge's sentence. It's a *promise* for our future. When Astra painted it, it wasn't to bring us together. We were *already* together! It was to remove obstacles from a destiny that we *both* already wanted. Remember what you said last night? That it couldn't be *just* for *my* benefit. If *you* hadn't wanted it, *La Manifestación* would never have worked."

That shut me up for a good minute. I'll be honest. Hearing that meant the world to me. "But the coming flood..." I said.

"Nicky, Earth as we know it will end in The Deluge – as it has before. But it will recover! *Los Hijos* means that you and I will survive the flood and grow old together here in Santa Fe.

Dios mío, how casually we discussed the coming apocalypse!

"Did you know Astra was bent on destroying the world?"

Daniel didn't bat an eye. "No, *guapo*. Now that you understand the extent of *mi madre's* secrets, you can also understand that I was out of the loop. I've told you about my non-contact with Tlaloceans. With the exception of *mi madre*, I've lived among humans exclusively since the late 1990s. I had rebelled against my parents, you see. And Astra knew not to ask me to join in her *Pintura Grande*, her final judgment. She knew I'd refuse as I've refused *every* request to succeed her as The Painter. *Mi madre* told you I was weak. But that wasn't it, Nicky. You know what it really was? After seeing a lifetime of Astra's pettiness, scheming and vindictiveness – much of which took place *decades* before there was any Zolteot threat–I simply couldn't reconcile myself to repeating her script, to being as flawed and fallible as I am and yet playing God."

A sound of thunder happened to roar at that precise moment. The rain on Astra's roof grew more intense. I pushed my hands against my ears. "That's what I can't live with!" I said too loudly. "Astra—playing God and destroying our world!"

Daniel looked at me with compassion. "That was my first reaction too when we saw her painting, *El Nuevo Mundo*. But the more I think about it, the more convinced I am that I was wrong. What if *mi madre* wasn't playing God? What if she was only an instrument and not truly the Final Judge?"

"But...she was a Judge-Priest. It was her job to judge."

He looked off into the distance. Thunder rumbled again. He said, "Yes. In the way that it is any judge's role to judge – to exercise discernment, to weigh facts, to manifest the transformation from what *is* into what *should* be. *Mira, guapo*....does the mere fact of discerning and then reacting mean that Astra actually played God? Well, maybe. Especially if you are convinced, the way I was, that she was acting alone with only her own caprices and wounds to guide her. But I've been wrong about so many things, Nicky. So many things. Now I'm thinking...what if Astra—like you and me – was simply playing her assigned part in advancing the destiny of the universe?"

"You're losing me."

"Nicky, consider the possibility that Astra's role was only a tiny one—a predestined one which she fulfilled as she was meant to—in an incomparably vast, all-encompassing *Pintura Grande*."

For a second, the rain and thunder receded into silence. My jaw dropped. A *Pintura Grande* vaster than... created by...? My mind couldn't comprehend it. "But the drowning of Earth! Astra's judgment!"

Daniel waved his finger at me. "Hold it! Is Astra destroying the Earth? Or is she *saving* it? Nicky, the Zolteots are not hypothetical enemies. They're here! On Earth now! Undercover, recruiting kapos, trying to destroy the will of human beings to fight them. And plotting the murder of all surviving Tlaloceans—including, might I remind you, your beloved husband."

Daniel spoke earnestly. "You yourself told me yesterday that the Zolteot fleet will be here in a matter of weeks. If they aren't stopped, there'll be nothing left. *Nada!* The oceans will disappear along with every drop of water on this planet. They will turn Earth into a desert where nothing will live but Zolteots and scorpions. Earth will become a dead cinder. Astra's way is better, isn't it? Living oceans? Islands? At least her judgment gives Earth a chance!"

Daniel's words perplexed me. "But Astra was so angry! So bitter!"

"Don't ever confuse anger for hate, Nicky." He spoke with deep emotion. "You can be terribly angry at someone and still love them and want to protect them. Parents do it all the time." His tone became pointed. "Spouses too."

I silently pondered these words, wondering if Astra was indeed Earth's destroyer or its savior. Was Daniel right? Was there an even grander *Pintura Grande*, its details fixed, within which these monumental events were just a small, predestined part?

I wandered over to the 18th Century altarpiece next to Astra's kiva. I brushed it lightly with my finger and closed my eyes. Life was so very strange.

Daniel came up behind me and put his hand on my shoulder. This time, nothing about his hand felt alien-strange. It was like the flesh and blood of an ordinary human struggling with extraordinary things. Which, of course, is already strange enough.

"Back at home, on the top shelf of our bookcase are the brushes and paint that *mi madre* left me," Daniel said. "Here in Astra's house there is more paint plus canvases. Given the collaborative effort *El Nuevo Mundo* must have taken, no surviving Judge-Priest—neither myself nor any stragglers who might remain—will be able to reverse her judgment. But you know something, Nicky? I can finally be the son that Astra always wanted! I'm not afraid to paint anymore! The blank islands in the painting! I can still make a difference..."

"But Daniel! Wouldn't that violate everything that made you rebel against Astra in the first place! *'La Vengadora?'* Vigilante justice?' 'The blood hatred of immortal fury?' How can you suddenly embrace the very things you said you despised? Aren't you just as flawed as you ever were? Yet now you're willing to play God?'"

Daniel looked as if I had just slapped his face. He closed his eyes but said nothing. With his acceptance of Astra's challenge, I had accused him of selling out. I wanted these words to hurt him. Despite my love for him, I wanted to cut him deep. To see if Tlaloceans bleed red.

But I also knew how unfair my words were. Daniel could never have foreseen how desperately the Tlalocean gift he had long abjured would now be needed to mitigate Astra's judgment. Yes, I was unfair, but I was confused and angry and done with all of this. Daniel watched me move to the door but did not react.

When I got to the door I turned and said, "Aren't you going to lock me in like your mother did?"

The pain and uncertainty that I saw in his face gradually resolved into something like serene acceptance. Of his mistakes. Of my ambivalence. Of his strange fate and the awesome responsibility he must now shoulder. When he spoke, Daniel's voice carried a maturity I had never before heard from him.

"No, Nicky," he said. "I will not lock you in. Not now, not ever. You are free to go out that door and no doors will ever be closed to you. Do you want to know why? After surviving 111 years of Astra de la Luz, I've learned that trying to force control on the people you love is the surest way to drive them away. And so, Man of Earth–husband, lover, best friend in a vast and lonely universe...I have faith that you'll always come back. From the moment I saw you across the room at that gallery gala staring at *El Hombre Que Canta*, I knew it was our destiny to be together. Not because of Astra, not because *Los Hijos* makes it so. But because the depth of love we feel for each other makes it so." He paused. "Do you not see the truth?"

I stopped short astonished. Love? Was it possible that it could all boil down to something as simple–as powerful–as universal–as that? A love so improbable it defied all of the usual expectations? I turned from the door to look at him and my heart leaped for a second. That fiery amber glint in Daniel's brown eyes–I suddenly realized that it wasn't the *alien* in him. It was the *love* in him. Authentic, deep love.

For the first time ever, I saw him. I saw the truth.

I felt numb–almost paralyzed—as Daniel came to me. He put his hand on my waist and shyly kissed me on the lips. I didn't try to avoid it, but I couldn't respond either. Could it ever be the same? Could it ever be right? I had the fleeting image of green-yellow scales and a lizard tongue housing an awesome, God-like power that I could neither share nor understand.

But when Daniel pulled back and looked at me with those handsome eyes that held just a trace of fire—my breath got short, I got butterflies in my stomach and—if you'll forgive my lack of delicacy in support of candor—I suddenly sported the most unexpected of erections. He had mentioned *El Hombre Que Canta*. How right he was. This alien being now standing before me was the same extraordinary young genius who had made me dizzy from wanting him 13 years ago when I first saw him standing behind the masterpiece which captured his raw, naked beauty in stone. Daniel Vigil Cruz! I loved him before we even exchanged a word. Not because of Astra. Our attraction, that ineffable drawing together, all happened *weeks* before Astra's painting of us had even been conceived of.

Suddenly, I felt as shy as I did on our first date when he was so suave, and I was drawn to him and I stammered from nervousness because I wanted him so much.

Then it dawned on me that I had just allowed Daniel, in his capacity as a revealed Tlalocean, to kiss me! This was our first coming together since he had shown me the truth. Before I understood what I was doing, I was kissing him back, passionately—biting at his lips, rubbing my body against his to see if he had the same physical reaction as me. He did. Oh, indeed he did.

When I stopped and looked at him, in my mind's eye I saw scales and flesh competing for dominance. I was repulsed and fascinated and scared. But mostly I was relieved. My body knew what my mind had not quite accepted. Daniel was still Daniel. I couldn't stop staring into his eyes as he gazed at me with a hunger which would have to wait.

But hold on! Was I going insane? How could this possibly work?

"*No hay miedo en el amor, Nicolás...*" Daniel answered me in his native tongue. No, I don't mean Tlalocean. Daniel was born *here*, in Santa Fe, Nuevo México. Before either Tlalocean or English, there was Spanish.

"There is no fear in love," I translated.

"*Claro*. No fear," Daniel answered as he pulled me into his arms and kissed me again.

He's right, I thought. Love. No fear. *But of all the men on Earth, why me?*

Again, he read my mind. He pushed me to arms length, took my left hand and gallantly kissed it. "Because you move me, Nicky. You move me."

PART IV: THE ARTIST

The rain is still pouring. There's a stream of water flowing down Aguas Dolores. I heard that there are electrical outages in Albuquerque. Denver and El Paso, too. This is getting real.

I'm back at my antique oaken writing desk. It's a little after 8:00 p.m. Daniel is back in the studio working. Ariel has eaten and had her muddy outside time. Now I think it's time for me to get back to writing. Believe it or not, I'm calm. Calmer than I was this morning or at any time since Astra died. So let me get back to the story. More specifically, Astra's house on Saturday.

Daniel called the number Astra had written down. A man named Hectór Martinez answered and said that he had been expecting Daniel's call. It would take him 40 minutes to get to Astra's since he lived up in Española with his granddaughter. While we waited, I asked Daniel more questions about his many years of living in the Tlalocean closet. He answered them patiently. Then Daniel stunned me with some quiet questions about my own history in the closet. I blushed recounting how I had dated Lorna Sanchez for five years and let her—and my parents—believe that I was straight and in love with her; even where there had never been any question in my mind that I was gay. That I was, in fact, sleeping with Tomás that last year without having the courage or decency to tell a soul—that is, until we were caught in the act together. Daniel had heard this story before, of course, and how it led to my banishment at the age of 23 and inspired my move to the freedom of San Francisco.

Daniel's wise. He didn't judge me. He didn't need to. He simply forced me to look at my own career of closeted, self-interested deception—my cowardly fear that others would discover who I really was. *Bravo*, Daniel. I mean it. He made his point and evened the score a little. More than a little. When I cowered in my closet, I was afraid to rock the boat. In contrast, Daniel's closet almost certainly saved lives.

When Hectór arrived, I was shocked. I had seen this man before! He was the same old man – worn out cowboy hat, grizzled skin, missing teeth - that I used to see hanging out at the Plaza playing mariachi songs on the violin for tourist coins. Despite his age, he looked strong as a bull. Funny. I had always thought he was some random homeless man—*un poco loco*, perhaps—who, nonetheless, had once been a good musician. These refugees from Tlaloc were full of surprises!

Hectór arrived as the passenger in a badly beat up green and yellow 2049 electrovan with tinted windows. The driver was a young brunette woman—attractive but diffident. She waved at me with a sad smile and made a head-bow to Daniel, who returned the gesture. She didn't get out and Hectór made no effort to introduce her. Once Hectór exited, Daniel directed the woman to move the van to the back of Astra's house.

Once out of sight of the street, the first thing Hectór did was bow deeply to Daniel. As he did so, he spoke words which were utterly impenetrable—somewhere in between Aztec and Xhosa, the clicking language from South Africa. Daniel was clearly embarrassed by Hectór's physical display of deference. As he responded with the same strange sounds, Daniel took Hectór's arm and bid him stand. Reverting to English, Daniel and Hectór exchanged a few words, mostly condolences about Astra. Then Daniel came over to me, took my hand firmly in his and introduced me to Hectór as his "husband and consort."

Hectór did not seem in the least bit surprised that Daniel had married a human, let alone an unambiguously (trust me) gay male. To the contrary. He took both of my hands in his, put them to his forehead and then smiled broadly saying "Con mucho gusto, mi buen amigo."

I nodded towards the young woman who drove the electrovan with a questioning expression.

"When she's ready," Hectór answered. "Her papa died recently. She's not ready to deal yet with..." He gestured towards the back door of the house. I said I understood.

Daniel put an arm on Hectór's shoulder. "Let's get out of the rain."

"Sí. Muchas gracias, Señor Jefe," Hectór said.

Daniel smiled at Hectór's unexpected use of the slang honorific. "Jefe" –pronounced hefay– basically means "boss man" in Mexican Spanish. I smiled too. I just may call Daniel that myself sometimes.

Hectór hesitated as he wiped his feet before entering the house. He pointed inside. "La Señora...Are you ready to let her go?"

Daniel looked at me and then nodded curtly. "Sí, mi amigo. Soy listo. I'm ready. Just tell me what to do."

"Jefe, you get her personal papers and anything from the homeworld that we don't want anyone to ask foolish questions about–or that could be misused by our enemies. You put them in a bag and take them home with you to be safe, entiendes?"

Daniel said he understood. He began to go through the house–primarily Astra's desk and–to my surprise–a safe she kept behind a painting in her bedroom. Apparently, Daniel knew the combination.

While Daniel was busy, Hectór asked me to help carry Astra's body to the back of the car. Instead of removing Astra's body from the blanket Daniel had wrapped her in, Hectór had me wait as he rolled her in a second blanket. We then carried my dear old friend, the artist, the witch – and my unexpected mother-in-law–Astra de la Luz, through the kitchen and out the back door to where Hectór's driver was waiting. I realized now why Daniel wanted the electrovan to be parked in back. He didn't want any random bystanders to see what looked like a couple of grave robbers at work.

Hectór didn't really need my help. Astra was so light. Cocooned as she was by two blankets, I never got to see if she had reverted to reptile form upon death. But I realized that it didn't make the least difference. There are some things that are none of our business, no?

Now that Astra's body was safe in the back of the van, it occurred to me that we were breaking the law. Now that I was a co-conspirator in the illegal movement of a corpse, I grew more concerned about the woman who sat in the electrovan's driver seat and who looked at me with frank curiosity.

"Aren't you going to introduce us?" I asked Hectór.

The woman took that as her cue to finally exit the van. Grabbing an umbrella against the light mist she thrust out her hand and said, "I'm Grace Martinez. Hectór's my grandpa."

Hectór in turn introduced me with a blend of Tlalocean, English and Spanish: *Nicolás, Tlacatl de Judge-Priest-Jefe- Daniel, Hijo de Astra"* which I inferred meant something like Nicholas, Husband of the Judge-Priest Boss-Man Daniel, Son of Astra."

"That's quite a title" Grace said with upraised eyebrows. She had a sweet voice with a slightly arch tone.

"Yeah. You can just call me Nick." Then I blurted out, "But I thought Tlaloceans..."

"Shhhhh," Hectór whispered. "She's not Tlalocean. She's human."

Grace added, "Born and bred in Española."

"But how...?"

Hectór suggested that the three of us sit on the steps of the covered back porch to get out of the drizzle.

"My wife Blanca and I were simple people on Tlaloc. Just peasants. We had no power, we were not artists. But we had friends who were able to help us escape *los cabrones Zolteots*." He turned and spit over the side of the porch. "Blanca and I tried to have children after we arrived on your planet. It was late in the migration–1948. We were never powerful Tlaloceans like Astra and José. But we were friends–even on Tlaloc. When they found out that we had escaped the destruction, they met us in Guadalajara and brought us here to *Nuevo México*.

"Astra was a very powerful Judge-Priest. Somehow, despite your..." he turned to Grace and asked, "how you say *campo magnético?*"

"Magnetic field," she offered.

"Despite Earth's magnetic field, Astra was able to conceive and bear a healthy child: your *tlacatl, el Jefe* Daniel. Blanca and I also tried to have children but...Earth's conditions made it impossible. I was grateful just to be alive, but my Blanca couldn't stand to be childless. Finally, after decades of crying for a child, Blanca and I did something that few other Tlaloceans did. We adopted a human baby boy from Las Cruces. Our son, Raymundo. He was a great man. No one could have made me prouder. Grace here is his daughter. She was born in 2035, so she's thirty-one—my only remaining relative."

Grace took her grandpa's hand. "I have the best grandpa you could ever hope for."

"Do you mind my asking what happened to Raymundo?" My question was insensitive and I regretted it at once.

Hectór cleared his throat and, for several seconds, appeared to study Astra's cottonwood and locust trees. "My Raymundito...He was born in 1990." Hectór's voice broke. He died last year from a heart attack. He was 76."

I expressed condolences to Hectór and Grace both. But *Dios mío*, as leathery as he was, Hectór himself didn't look like he was more than 75!

"Grace knows all about you then?"

Grace interjected. "Of course I do, Nick. I'm not that slow. Grandpa's lived with me since before my dad passed. It wasn't that hard to figure out that I was living with someone...rather different. I asked questions and demanded answers."

I have to admit that Grace made me feel a bit stupid. How was it possible that I never suspected anything out of the ordinary? I've lived with Daniel as my husband for over 12 years! Well, maybe it goes to Daniel's skill at dissembling...*Ay*. Forget it. Sore subject.

Hectór patted Grace on the back lightly. "Grace knows everything about me, *mi amigo*. Everything." He lowered his voice conspiratorially. "What can we poor Tlaloceans do if we don't have a few humans we can trust?"

At that point, Daniel reemerged from the house. He was done retrieving documents and objects from Tlaloc that might incriminate Astra or him should the Zolteots—or the coroner— snoop around. It was time to move on. Hectór, Grace and I left the porch and stood by the electrovan.

After Grace was properly introduced to Daniel, Hectór took off his wet cowboy hat and held it before him as a gesture of respect. "*Jefe*, before we go, I have a favor to ask."

Daniel nodded his head. "Anything, Hectór."

Hectór opened the back door of his van. On the seat was a blank canvas. How did he know? Astra must have told him her plans in advance.

"My granddaughter, Grace..." He nodded to his granddaughter and handed a photograph to Daniel. "I don't care about myself, you understand. I've had a good long life."

I put my hand to my mouth. Is this what Daniel's future meant? I had to fight back tears.

Daniel gave Hectór a hug. "Come back Monday morning. It'll be done."

Hectór bowed and then moved towards the passenger door. "*Bueno. I'll be...*"

Daniel called out, "*¡Uno momento, Hectór!*"

Hectór stopped. "*Sí, Jefe?*"

"Let me take a picture of you and Grace. Together. For when I paint you."

I don't know if it was rain or tears that trickled down Hectór's face. "*Muchas gracias, Jefe.*"

Daniel took a picture of them with their arms around each other. It was a fine picture because... well, that picture meant the difference between life and death. In a day or so it would be transformed by the artist's hand into something that would save Grace and her grandpa from a watery grave.

Just before they left, Grace came over to me and gave me a spontaneous hug. "Do you even know what a brave man you are, Nick? Listen. You have grandpa's number. Here's our address in Española." She wrote it down for me. "Call me when you need to. If the phones go out—*when* the phones go out—at least you'll know how to find us. There aren't many of us humans who are connected to Tlaloc or have any idea what's really going on. Your husband bears a heavier burden than I can imagine. You may need someone to talk to."

I thanked her. Twice.

Yes, Daniel and I were alone. But no longer quite so alone.

I never did find out where Hectór and Grace planned to take Astra. To some unknowable Tlalocean field of the dead, I imagine. It was only as I watched them make their left turn onto Aguas Dolores that I even remembered it was Halloween.

It no longer mattered. All masks had been removed.

It's 10:00 p.m. now. Of course it's still raining. Daniel wants me to come to bed. I told him I'd be there in just a few minutes. I've been opening the window off and on – I'm trying to hear whether the rainwater is draining into the *acequia*. I know our property should be safe, but... A few minutes ago I heard the bells chime from St. Francis Cathedral. Why now? A warning of some kind? *What tale of terror, now, their turbulency tells? Ay*, just slap me. The last thing I need to think about now is Edgar Allen Poe. Let me just finish this journal so I can move forward! Let it be done with so I... so I can talk to Daniel before he falls asleep.

Back to Saturday. After Astra's body was taken away, Daniel put a suitcase full of her potentially incriminating papers and Tlalocean relics into the trunk of his car. Then Daniel and I got in our separate cars to return home. *El Nuevo Mundo* would remain at Astra's – for now – but Daniel took *Los Hijos* with him. He drove on ahead. For a fleeting moment I thought of driving in the opposite direction, far, far away. I suppose the choice to leave will always be on the table. But the storm had come and home needed to be where Daniel was. His art studio. Ariel. My antique oaken desk.

The rain was strong and steady now, the sky as grey as death.

Lightning lit up the Sangre de Cristos. I heard the rumble of thunder. Puddles had begun to accumulate. I shuddered. Who could say what horrors lay ahead?

Now that I was alone in my car, I thought about *El Nuevo Mundo*. Earth would be 95% covered in water. But Astra had left blank islands as dry land. With Daniel's gift—*La Manifestación*—those islands could be filled with trees and flowers, with museums and monuments, with elephants and birds...and people. I thought about Hector and Grace. Would other Tlalocean commoners—all of whom lacked the powers that Daniel possessed—come begging for the gift of life through his art? Was he truly the last surviving Judge-Priest?

Of course he was. Now I finally recognized the wisdom and forethought of Astra excluding Daniel from the final *Manifestación*. She knew that the energy-burden of manifesting *El Nuevo Mundo* would kill all of the Judge-Priests who participated. She didn't dare risk her son. She truly loved him. And If Daniel had died, who would be left to paint Earth's survival?

I pictured each of those blank spots Astra had deliberately left on the watery globe. None of them were recognizable islands or features. But that didn't matter. Daniel could turn those blank spots on Astra's painting into something better than Noah's Ark had ever been. Through the power of Daniel's art, much of nature, culture—and humanity could be saved!

I realized in that moment how much vaster this was than just me and my neurosis. This was about the survival of every terrestrial thing we cared about! Grace was right. Daniel now bore an unimaginable burden. This son of Tlaloc—my artist husband—was supremely important!

When I entered the home I shared with this Tlalocean being, Ariel greeted me with jumps and licks. Then I looked up and saw Daniel gazing at me with that glint of fire in his eyes. He had already propped *Los Hijos* up on the mantle over the kiva where we would eventually hang it. And with the next clap of thunder, even as I began to shake with fear, Daniel broke into a triumphant grin.

Later that evening, when it became clear that there would be no trick-or-treaters due to the harsh weather, I entered Daniel's studio. He was busy painting. He grunt-nodded to me with a brush in his mouth and paint-stains on his Armani shirt. He had completed *Nuestra Calle* that afternoon. Now he was bouncing back and forth between two paintings: one was his promised portrait of Hectór and Grace. The other appeared to be the outlines of the Basilica San Marco and the adjacent piazza in Venice.

I wandered over to the sculpture he had been working on for the last year--that male-pursuing-male reimagining of Bernini's *Apollo and Daphne*. In the sensitive work of Daniel's hand and chisel I saw my own face sculpted into Apollo and I saw the man I was pursuing frozen in the act of changing into something nonhuman. Here was tension, attraction, fear, sensuality and resolve, all locked together forever in marble. Was this necessarily a frightening thing? I finally understood the painful but absolute beauty it depicted.

That was Saturday. On Sunday, while Daniel worked, I went to the grocery store and stocked up enough supplies for a month. Beyond that, we'll have to trust the powers that be. I also went to a fishing and tackle megastore. You know what I bought? A little motorboat. It has green and yellow trim. I took that as a sign. It just barely fit on the ski rack on my car's roof. When I showed it to Daniel he laughed at me. He said we wouldn't need it. But I like to hedge my bets. Makes sense, no?

Today was Monday – actually, it still is for another two hours. Hectór and Grace came by early this morning to pick up their painting,

Verdaderos Amigos—"True Friends." It came out beautifully. How very grateful they both were. I had a nice heart-to-heart with Grace. She reminds me of a young version of Astra—minus the vindictive telekinesis. A sharp wit, flamboyant clothes. We could be friends in another life. Actually, maybe there's still time in this one. With the protection imparted by Daniel's gift, Hectór and Grace will survive the Deluge. Who knows when Daniel and I will see them again, but... *Dios mío*, what the hell am I saying? Of *course* we'll see them again. We'll make a point of it!

But that's in an uncertain future. Just getting through today is hard enough. Today was the *Dia de Los Muertos*. There's flood water in the *acequia* and Daniel and I are alone on this strange, beleaguered planet in a way that's unimaginable. I spent hours today sitting here with Ariel looking out at the world, but with all the mist I could no longer see the Sangre de Cristos. *Ay*, this rain is really pouring. I just watched the news. Even with power outages and flood advisories being reported from different parts of the world, no one seems to realize the implications of all this rain just yet. But they will.

The implications... Do you realize there are over 10 billion human souls on this planet? How many of them do you think will survive this? *Jesús Cristo*, my hand has begun to shake again. I dare not think such thoughts. My sanity is too fragile.

May I confess something to you? Despite Daniel's protection and all that I've learned about Tlaloc and Judge-Priests and *La Manifestación*, I'm still scared beyond words. I can't begin to imagine the destruction that has already begun out there. I hear the *Dies Irae* from the Requiem Mass echoing and echoing in my head. I hear a thousand choirs silenced one singer at a time until there is only deathly quiet. *Dios, Dios, Perdóname*. Forgive me that I live when so many will die.

I'm going to cry for a little bit now. *Ay*. I've cried more in the last three days than I ever thought possible.

Alright, I'm better now. Listen. I feel survivor's guilt and terrible grief. But I'm also selfish. Can you blame me that I'm grateful to be safe with Daniel? I'm deeply grateful – even if I'm somewhat disturbed by the bizarre creature that hides beneath his handsome exterior.

Daniel and I made love last night. I didn't initiate it and I wasn't sure I could even rise to the occasion. How could I? After I was exposed to the unutterable complexity lurking beneath that flawless skin, the idea of sex scared the hell out of me. But the lights were out, the rain was pounding on the roof and the warmth of Daniel's body next to mine gave me solace. Plus I was curious. It somehow felt safe in the dark to resume the explorations I had started on Saturday when his flesh had erupted into scales.

This time when I made the same exploration of his body, instead of reptile scales his flesh – and mine – erupted into throbbingly human male arousal. There was something about wrestling in bed with a dangerously mysterious scion of Tlalocean royalty that really inflamed me. As the excitement built, it ultimately exploded into a climactic ecstacy I never thought possible.

Is this too much information? *Lo siento mucho.* I'm sorry, but it's the truth.

When we were done, I was utterly exhausted. He had both filled and drained me. I found myself more in love than I ever could have imagined..

Daniel fell asleep almost instantly. As he softly snored, I laid my head on his chest and wrapped my arm around his warm flesh. I listened for that heartbeat in triplets, but I never heard it. I looked over at his sleeping face and briefly thought that he looked like an angel. Then I remembered the reptile scales and the lizard tongue. Well, who's to say

96

what an angel is supposed to look like?

Then I breathed deeply of Daniel. He was scented with a melange of our sexual collision, Pierre Cardin, almonds and just a trace of oil paint. I love him. *Dios mío*, how I love him. But when fitful sleep finally came, I dreamt of dragons and dinosaurs. So what? I'm only human. God, I'm only human.

When Daniel and I were first dating–when I was that nerdy art critic for the San Francisco rags and he was *El Escultor*–we went to San Francisco's Legion of Honor Museum. As we held hands and viewed masterpiece after masterpiece, Daniel talked to me about the art of sculpting. Since the days of Ancient Greece, he said, the greatest artists have asserted that the sculpture waits inside the marble waiting to be released by chisel and hammer. But Daniel said this wasn't true – at least not for him. Daniel said that the sculptor doesn't *release* what's inside. He crafts a stone temple which *guards* what's inside. Think of that! The statue's essence is protected forever in a temple of marble. I didn't understand him then. But I do now.

I thought of that story after we made love. I rolled my hand across Daniel's bare chest in wonder–gently, so as not to wake him. Like a sculptural masterpiece, this smooth, bronzed veneer was a temple which protected Daniel's essence. When all was said and done, what difference was there between Daniel and the way my soul was protected by my own veneer of flesh?

I have more to say. Daniel has taught me something important about angels and devils. Severo Lopez, the kapo who killed José de la Luz–he was a devil. The Zolteots are devils. Those humans who gleefully collaborate with evil in hopes of profit? *Diablos puros*. The worst sort of monsters. But Daniel? Not on your life. True, I will never forget the fire-eyed dragon who rumbled at me in Astra's parlor. But is there a reason why I should fear something I will never see again? What earthly good could that possibly accomplish? With the world ending, there are literally a thousand things to consider which matter more!

I still burn a little that Daniel held the truth hostage from me for so long. But I have to triage what's important. Even as this corrupt chapter of Earth's history ends, it's Daniel's gift of life which gives me hope. The blank islands that Astra purposefully left in her great painting, *El Nuevo Mundo*, also give me hope—as does the idea that there is an even greater *Pintura Grande* somewhere out there.

Tomorrow will be a new day. Daniel and I will wake up together. He'll go to work and I'll look out through the pouring rain at Daniel's studio in the *casita* and my fear will be tempered with gratitude. For so long as the Deluge allows, Daniel will use Astra's brushes and pigments and his own formidable talent to paint everything and anything that he would save. Never has his art been more consequential. Never have I been prouder of the man I call my husband.

Readers of this journal... If you exist at all, how are you going to judge me? What do *you* think I should have done? Despite Astra and the paintings of Tlaloc I still believe in free will. Should I have chosen to drown to death in solidarity with a debased humanity that has collaborated in its own destruction? Or am I right to choose life with someone who has loved me well for over twelve years? Whose lack of humanness matters far less than his exceptional sense of humanity. Someone who can paint. Someone whose gifts as Astra's heir may allow, not for the survival of the fittest, but for the survival of the *best*.

An old world is passing away and a new world will soon begin. Is it not my duty to stick with Daniel as we—reluctantly—take on the roles of Mr. and Mr. Noah? I believe that it is. But understand something. For me, it is not *just* a duty. Can you not see the truth? To be with my

Tlalocean husband is the privilege of a lifetime.

But as the flood waters rise and Daniel works furiously to fill our metaphoric Ark with paintings that are so much more than paintings, I'm left to wonder: who and what of our old world will Tlaloc's last surviving Judge-Priest decide deserves to survive? And how will Daniel's strange, miraculous gift shape the New World to come?

THE END

CPSIA information can be obtained
at www.ICGtesting.com
Printed in the USA
BVHW040508070622
639033BV00003B/253